I0533161

Copyright ©2013 by Traci M Sanders

Cover design by 4WillsPublishing. To learn more please visit their website at

www.4willspublishing.worpress.com

The author's intent in providing this story is only to entertain you. The characters and events are fictional.

When Darkness Breaks

By Traci M Sanders

Prologue

The sun beamed down on the freshly-cut grass, with not a single cloud in sight. A gentle breeze brushed the faces in the crowd. Annie's team led by two points in the last game of the season. She had begged her father to let her play center forward. "Please, Daddy. I know I can score a goal. Give me a chance to show you." Drake was a sucker for those teddy bear eyes and had agreed to let her try.

Annie's little brother, Max, busied himself with matchbox cars, on a blanket situated next to his mother.

With only two minutes left in the game, Amber scanned the soccer field and quickly located her husband, Drake. She admired how compassionate and patient he was as a coach; but her heart truly melted when she watched him interact with their daughter, Annie. In fact, Drake's propensity to be a good father was what had attracted Amber to him from the moment they first met.

A smile emerged on her face as she reflected on that day.

~

It was a hot July afternoon. Ice cream trucks and squeals of little children serenaded the town. Amber had just graduated college and worked at waiting tables for extra income. The diner was nearly desolate but a bit overstaffed. Drake walked in with two little girls stuck to his legs, and chose a seat in Amber's station. He sported a pair of dark jeans and a solid green muscle shirt that hugged the curves of his biceps. Amber's eyes were fixed on paper in hand while she took their order, in an attempt to disguise the warm, crimson glow on her cheeks.

As the girls enjoyed their after-meal vanilla cone, Amber stood alone at the counter. Her fingers twirled tiny strands of hair. Boredom was clearly written all over her face, until Drake invited her to join them. She learned that he was en route to the movie theatre with his two nieces. As she watched him interact with the girls, Amber became convinced that he was quality 'daddy' material. That was a very important item on her checklist, since she had never known her own father.

She smiled and listened intently while Drake described his life as an architect at a local design firm. The passion he had for his job excited her, as she was career-driven too. Every word he spoke slid off his tongue effortlessly, the way sweat trickled down the outer edges of an icy soda bottle on a hot summer day. She melted in every place that counts when he looked at her with those chocolate brown eyes, sprinkled with tiny flecks of green. Five years her senior, Drake had a certain aura about him that made her feel safe. Every time he smiled at her, she felt like the only woman in the world. No man had ever had that effect on her.

Amber didn't date much but told herself she would instantly *know* when the right man came along. Though the timing was severely premature, she had already allowed herself to envision what life would be like with him.

Before he left the diner, Drake asked for her number. Three dates later, the two were nearly inseparable.

***

Just six months into their relationship, Drake took Amber back to the diner where they met, and proposed. The wedding took place outside a small chapel in their home-town of Wichita. He promised Amber a dream wedding as soon as they could afford it. The couple exchanged vows with simple gold bands, purchased from a local pawn shop, but what those infinite circles signified had more importance for Amber than their appearance or cost.

Jill, Amber's mother, attended the nuptials, with some reluctance. Amber's father had been killed in the war when she was a small child, so for as long as she could remember, it was just the two of them. No man would ever be good enough for Jill's little girl, and she definitely didn't trust the smooth-talking Drake Woods. Most of all, she couldn't stand to see her daughter be subservient to a man. She'd raised Amber to be a confident, self-sufficient woman like herself, but when Drake was around, *that* girl disappeared.

Amber had always dreamed of becoming a world renowned journalist and traveling to other countries to interview foreign leaders. But after she steadily worked her way up the proverbial corporate ladder, from producer's assistant to weekend anchor, those dreams got put on hold—when Amber announced she was pregnant. She stayed home with her daughter for six months then went back to work, and Annie was placed in full-time day care.

For the next year, Amber proved her worth time and again to the station manager. The money was good, and her new nickname at the station was "the go-to gal," because she covered every story she could get her hands on. Things were going well for Drake too. The higher-ups had taken notice of his talent.

By the age of one, Annie had suffered several colds and sinus infections. Drake and Amber realized it was due to her interactions with the multitude of kids at the day care center. They agreed it was best if one of them stayed home with her full time. Drake worked out a deal with his office, which allowed him to come in once a week to pick up projects, and complete them from home. It was the perfect arrangement.

Almost three years later, the Woods welcomed a nine pound, seven ounce baby boy to their family. Amber took only six weeks leave from the station then returned to work.

Drake became a stay-home dad. He had been raised in a family of four boys, and his father coached his soccer team and managed the home, while his mom ran her own ballet studio.

Since Drake was always with the kids, Jill rarely spent any time with her grandchildren, another thing she resented him for. Though she was relieved when the couple bought a house just one mile down the street from her. At least she still had her daughter close by.

~

Amber's mind returned to the moment. She cheered as Annie scored the winning goal to finish the game. Afterwards, the four of them went out to celebrate, complete with hot dogs and ice cream—Annie's favorites.

At home, they hung out in the backyard until the sun sank behind the trees. The night concluded with popcorn and a movie in the den, until both kids were fast asleep, piled atop their parents. Drake carried the children to their beds then made his way to his own, where Amber lay dressed in nothing but a hungry smile. They locked the door and made out like teenagers who were out past curfew on a school night. It was sweet, passionate, and after all those years, still amazing.

***

That was once pretty much the course of events on any given Saturday for the Woods family, until … tragedy struck, and the life Amber knew, ceased to exist.

Chapter One

How It All Began

Excitement made Amber jittery, despite the delicious anniversary meal she and Drake had just shared at the local bistro. She had big news. That morning, the station had offered her a promotion, and wanted to move her to Seattle, where she would be the head anchorwoman for the Channel 6 Seattle Beat. This would mean the entire family would need to transfer there with her.

What an incredible opportunity for her. It would mean much more money for the family. Drake had always supported Amber's career, and was proud of her. But, that particular night, she had discovered he had news of his own.

Not wanting to fight in the restaurant, they waited until they left and were headed to the babysitter's house to pick up the children. Amber had hoped they'd be done before they had little ears in the back of the car, but the argument just grew more and more heated.

"What do you mean?" She frowned and fiddled with her seatbelt.

"They want to send me to New York. I'll be leading a team in the design of the new International Science Building. It's the opportunity of a lifetime ... Why can't you be happy for me?"

"But, … what about my job? My career. Didn't you hear how big a chance this is for me? For us?"

"What about mine? It's always about you. You and your job. You and your career. You. You. You. …"

Amber huddled in the passenger seat, her head pressed against the window, and tried to ignore Drake's anger and disappointment. He wasn't the only one who felt hurt and let down. He'd always supported her, so why would he change his mind now? Right when she had her big chance?

The engine roared as he put his foot down, and the gravity pushed Amber back into the seat.

"Slow down!" she yelled.

"God, you are such a control freak. I'm sick of you telling me what to do." He slammed the wheel with the heel of his palm. "I thought you'd understand. I love being a stay-home-dad, but this is a chance I can't pass up."

Amber crossed her arms. She loved her children but did *not* want to be a stay-home-mom. Especially not now. The car lurched and shuddered, and produced a sickening crunch followed by a bang. The tires squealed when Drake slammed on the brakes, and metal screeched on metal—the sound was ear-splitting.

"What happened?"

Drake ignored her, and muttered an expletive under his breath. He jumped out of the car as soon as it stopped. The kids wailed and screamed in the back seat. Amber's heart raced as she unbuckled her seat belt and turned to tend to them. God, couldn't this have happened before they'd collected them from the sitter's?

Five-year-old Annie was inconsolable. "Mommy, it was a boy, bigger than me. Daddy hit him."

Amber's heart nearly stopped. Frantic, she leapt from the car and ran to where her husband knelt on the wet asphalt. A crowd had already gathered, and stood in shocked silence.

In the distance, sirens blared and flashing blue lights drew nearer. Amber looked back at her husband, who was administering CPR to the young boy. The kid's bike lay crumpled and smashed about three feet away. Annie and Max's screams reached her from the car, but everything sounded like it was under water.

"No. No, no, no." Drake whispered over and over again.

The emergency services arrived, and relieved Drake from his efforts. A few minutes later, the police arrived and wanted to take statements. Numb, Amber tried to cooperate with a young officer, while also trying to calm her hysterical children.

Reporters showed up at their house and camped out every day, demanding statements. Amber refused to give them anything they could use against her—being well aware of how the 'business' worked. She couldn't even make a trip to the grocery store without being followed or bombarded by cameras in the parking lot. She didn't want to show her face in the neighborhood, let alone on television. So, she turned down the Seattle offer and quit her job. Amber hid out at home, while Drake sought refuge at his office. After a few weeks, they put their house up for sale, and Drake accepted the job in New York. It didn't matter that the young boy had been riding in the dark without lights or reflectors, or that the police hadn't pressed charges. She and Drake had ended a twelve-year-old kid's life.

The house sold in two weeks. It saddened Amber to let it go. This was the first home she and Drake had bought together—a two story brick, with beautiful bay windows in front, a winding staircase in the entrance, and a huge eat-in kitchen. Annie and Max had both learned to walk on those floors. She and Drake had christened every room inside. And it was the only home both of her children had ever known.

Best of all, her mother lived right down the street. But, when she thought about all the bad memories wrapped up in that town, Amber agreed a move to New York might be the fresh start they needed. Although, it didn't take long for them to realize they couldn't outrun their problems.

Chapter Two

Welcome to New York

Drake's company had all of their belongings shipped to the new residence, which took a lot of stress from their family. In addition, he was provided with a company car, an expense account, and a beautiful furnished home in an upscale neighborhood, about ten miles from downtown. Though Drake soon realized that the commute was much longer with traffic.

It took about three weeks for Amber to get everything unpacked and put away. The house was nice, but definitely didn't have the comfortable feel of their home in Kansas. It seemed all of their neighbors were stuffy rich people who rarely made an appearance during the day, other than to exit their garages, en route to work or fancy restaurants. Some of the women were stay-home moms like Amber, but they already had their own neighborhood cliques established. Amber surmised that most of them probably worked in fancy Manhattan offices, as she took note of how they were dressed.

Sometimes, she missed the corporate life. She no longer had a reason to don makeup or a pair of high heels. Well, for longer than a session of dress-up with her daughter anyway. But, when she looked into her children's eyes, Amber was right where she never knew she always wanted to be.

For a while, it seemed the move was just what they needed. Mr. Shelton put Drake to work right away on the Science Building project, which meant a lot of late nights away from his wife and kids. But it kept him distracted enough to not dwell on the past. Usually, Amber waited up for Drake, no matter how late. She asked him all about his day, while he devoured a re-warmed dinner. It seemed redundant and boring to Drake, but his wife absorbed every word he said. It was the only adult conversation she was afforded during the day.

After dinner, they kissed the kids goodnight then slipped off to their room and made love for hours. Even if Drake had to get up early the next day, they always made time for each other.

***

Annie attended an exclusive private school, which Drake's company also helped pay for. A good education was very important to both Amber and Drake.

Amber enjoyed her time with Max during the day, but soon realized that toddlers weren't an adequate substitute for adult interaction. There was only so much house cleaning she could do in a day, and so many ways to redecorate without overdoing it. She was very supportive of her husband and knew he was doing what was needed to take care of their family, but soon the pressures of taking care of two children alone wore on her.

Amber decided to join a local gym. Yoga had been her go-to sport for relaxation and staying in shape back in Kansas. She saw an ad on television for the Yoga Mania studio, which was about a block away, and decided to give it a try. By the end of three classes, she was hooked, and happy to have found an outlet to help release some stress.

***

There were definitely perks to living in a big city. She could have an entire nutritious dinner delivered to their door within thirty minutes, which included a fresh salad. At first, Amber was excited to have so many amazing opportunities for the children. The neighborhood held a multitude of unique places to shop, Central Park was beautiful and serene, and the streets were alive with performers. But, soon the new wore off, and for the first time in her life, Amber had a surplus of money and time at her disposal, yet she was not happy.

***

About six months after the couple arrived in New York, things went downhill for Drake. While on his way home from work one evening, he passed a terrible auto accident that involved a little boy. The scene vividly brought the past back to him. His work nights got later and later, and Amber wondered if he was actually *at* the office. He often reeked of liquor and women's perfume—not a scent that belonged to his wife. She learned that his office building had a sports gym inside, and noticed he had been working out. Though *she* had not benefited from his new sexy physique in quite some time.

Amber didn't recognize her husband or her life anymore. She felt like a single parent. Even the teachers at Annie's school inquired about her marital status a few times for parental events. When Drake did show up to school functions, it never went well, and they fought about it for days afterwards. It definitely wasn't the life she had imagined, but she held to the ongoing promise from Drake that things would calm down "as soon as the project was finished."

Sometimes, she grew homesick and missed her mother terribly. They spoke on the phone at least once per day. Though she tried to put on a façade, Jill could tell when something was wrong with her daughter. The conversations always seemed to be the same:

"Honey, is everything okay with you and Drake?"

"Everything's fine, Mom, he just has to work a lot. It's a new job and things will settle down soon." She was trying to convince herself more than her mother.

"Well, call me if you need me, and you know you always have a place to go."

"I don't want my kids to grow up without a father like I did, Mom. Drake loves us and is doing all of this for us. I want to support him."

The conversation ended with Amber feeling exasperated, as always, from having to explain away her husband's recent lack of presence in their family. Amber would often find an excuse to cut the conversation short, usually something that involved the kids. Then mother and daughter exchanged phone kisses and promised a call for the next day.

Chapter Three

Happy Anniversary

Amber tried to melt her worries in the hot, soapy pool of heaven she had just stepped into, but the day's events ran through her restless mind like a soundtrack stuck on repeat, even as the warm cloth covered her eyes. What was Drake doing that was more important than sharing that rare stolen moment with her?

***

Amber had planned the perfect night for the two of them. The champagne sat on ice, a romantic movie waited in the DVD player, and she had even cooked a tender rack of lamb with rosemary garnish from scratch. She and the kids had spent most of the morning at the park to ensure they would be tired enough to meet with an early bedtime. Her hair was curled, her skin shaven and moisturized—even her makeup was done—which, these days, was unusual. The shopping trip to the local boutique had proven successful because she found a short, red strapless cocktail dress that fit her firm body like a glove.

Candles flickered and sexy music played as Amber sipped on a glass of wine—she wanted to open the champagne with Drake. Then, she sat and anticipated what would transpire in the moments to come.

But *hours* later, when the food was cold and the champagne was hot, it became heartbreakingly apparent that he had forgotten their anniversary (again).

Amber sipped on the no-longer-bubbly drink alone, and finally relaxed in the tub, until her nose was just above water. The screech of truck tires in the driveway brought her back to the surface.

Gravel had scattered into the neighbor's yard. Drake cursed and stumbled up the front steps to a locked door. Unable to locate his keys, he beat on it with clenched fists ... bang, bang, bang. Amber sprang from the tub, threw her gown on, and hurried to let him in before he woke the little ones.

"Why the hell did you lock the door, woman?" he bellowed at her.

Amber had come to expect moments like these, over the past few years, especially on their anniversary, but never really got used to it. She looked at him with a mixture of disgust and empathy, because she knew what had made him that way. Deep down, even though she detested his behavior, she longed to hold him and tell him everything would be okay. To let him know that he was still the man she loved. But in the heat of that moment, pain and anger overcame her.

"Quiet or you'll wake the kids, you drunken fool!" She presented her words in a loud whisper. "Where have you been?" She completely avoided his question about the locked door.

"Nowhere that concerns you." His voice sounded cold and condescending. He threw her a slight grin, and for a moment, she imagined a hint of concern in his eyes. Perhaps he had noticed the disappointment and hurt written on her face, because his demeanor softened a bit, but no—it only mocked.

"Aw, come on, baby. You wanna climb in daddy's lap and tell him all about *your* night?" He traced her soaking wet auburn hair to the ends and wrapped his fingers around the spaghetti straps of her silk lavender nightie, then continued downward toward her soft, perky breasts.

Even years later, at six feet two inches, Drake's two-hundred pound, non-chiseled-yet-not-flabby frame, made him the perfect hot-dad type it seemed all the women in town wanted. And apparently *at least one* had been successful that night. His clothes were disheveled, his hair tousled, and the aroma of Chanel No. 5 hung in the air. He used to buy the same perfume for her. Despite knowing all that, it took everything she had to resist his touch.

She slapped his hand away in an attempt to show her disgust.

"You're a bit too late. I've already taken care of *myself* tonight." Her words were meant to be sharp, but she hoped he didn't hear the obvious cry for attention in her voice. "Why don't you go find whoever put that ridiculous smile on your face tonight and finish your good time?"

Drake smiled and winked, then said, "Well, at least it would get done right, then."

Amber slapped his cheek so hard the sting rushed to her fingertips like fire. She turned toward the bedroom and Drake followed. She slammed the door in his face as she called out from the other side, "Happy Anniversary to you too, jackass!"

Drake's footsteps thumped along the hardwood floor in an uneven, heavy tread toward the living room.

Amber lay in bed and reminisced about the way things used to be on their anniversary. Drake always met her at the door with champagne, purple roses, and a rack-of-lamb dinner that infused the entire house with flavor. It had become their tradition. He *always* remembered their anniversary and took months to plan his next big surprise for her. Of course, that was all before the … no, she didn't want to go to sleep thinking about that. Her plan of recreating their happy moments had failed miserably, again.

Thoughts raced through her mind as hot tears streamed down her mascara-painted face. She ran her hands over her abs and thighs, and noticed a little less cushion than before. The yoga classes were paying off. She wasn't supermodel hot, but her five-feet-six-inch frame was still pretty easy on the eyes. In fact, Amber had embraced her womanly curves that resulted from birthing two children.

Drake used to worship her body, but she could barely recall the last time he touched her with more passion than a peck on the lips, before he left for work. She hugged her pillow tighter, and felt inadequate. Who had she become? She was once a bright shining star that everyone was drawn to. Until Drake came along, she had never put much stock into what a man thought of her. How could she give away all of her power like that?

Amber wanted to call and cry to her best friend Janie, whom she had met several months ago in yoga class, but it was much too late at night.

Janie stood at five feet, eight inches with the body of a goddess. She had naturally curly, chestnut hair, seemingly ageless skin, and eyes bluer than the ocean. Though she denied it, Amber was sure her friend had been a model at some point.

The two women hit it off right away. Janie was married with two kids as well, but her husband frequently worked out of town, which allowed the friends a lot of time together. They drank coffee and exchanged the latest developments of their favorite television drama series. It helped that the kids enjoyed playing together. Thank God for Janie. She was Amber's only true friend in a town she resented for taking her husband away.

Amber wiped her eyes and released a heavy sigh. Tomorrow would be another day, and she had to face Drake eventually. Just before she drifted off to sleep, she hoped he would have a huge red mark across his left cheek in the morning. Maybe then he would feel even a little bit of the pain that consumed her.

Chapter Four

The Day After

The smell of bacon, eggs, and coffee awakened Drake sooner than he'd hoped. The kids were fighting over which Saturday morning cartoon to watch.

He looked over, still sleepy, at Amber, who took control of the situation. "Annie, you and your brother need to find something both of you can agree on, or I am going to turn the television off completely." Her tone was kind but firm.

Daylight blinded Drake as it spilled through the living-room curtains. He grabbed his pillow and stumbled to his bed, where he slept off the better part of the day. He didn't even hear the door slam when Amber and the kids left.

***

After a sultry day at the soccer field, Amber headed to Janie's house to let the kids hang out and cool off in the pool.

Janie's backyard was like a small resort in its own right. It had a beautiful stone-paved patio that encircled the luxury swimming pool, with a built-in waterslide in the middle. So much foliage surrounded them that it felt like a tropical paradise to Amber. It had one of those fancy barbeque grills on the right, adjacent to an island bar, which plush swivel stools lined. To the left, a playground had everything to entertain small children, from trapeze bars, to rock climbing walls, and a sand pit beneath. Janie preferred to go to the park most of the time because she felt cut off from the world in her backyard, but the kids reveled in the refreshing water on their skin that day.

"So, I didn't hear back from you last night. Things must have gone well with the anniversary dinner. Was Drake surprised?" Janie settled into the plush lounge chair next to Amber and handed her a strawberry daiquiri. Since her husband Brad, mostly focused on the kids when he came home on the weekends, Janie was often left to *take care of herself* as well. She was eager to hear even the slightest sexy detail about Amber's night.

Brad and Janie were in love and very committed to their relationship, but it wasn't what one would call passionate. Amber had never really seen them kiss, and Janie didn't speak much about their sex life. When she did talk about her husband, she mostly referred to his fathering qualities. Amber didn't push the subject. Her own relationship wasn't a walk in the park, and she would have given anything for Drake to be an involved father again.

Brad made good money and obviously wanted to give his wife everything possible. He even bought an extra spa certificate once so Janie and Amber could enjoy a relaxing day together, without the kids. Though her husband was just trying to provide her a much needed break, what she really wanted was a night of unbridled passion with her man. That was another reason she and Amber got along so well. Just like Brad, even when Drake was at home, he wasn't always *there*.

"Not quite."

Janie squinted when she detected the disappointment in Amber's voice. "He had apparently done some *celebrating* of his own before he made it home."

"What an asshole."

"Whatever, I'm getting used to it."

"Girl, you deserve so much better than him." Janie reached over and offered her friend a supportive hand on the shoulder. "Is there anything I can do?"

"No, I'm sure he'll come around soon. We've been through a lot together and I'm not ready to give up on him just yet. But you are right, he is an asshole." Both women laughed uncontrollably, and almost spilled their drinks.

The rum offered a slight buzz, but Amber had to drive home, so they stopped at just one drink. And, just to be safe, she hung around for a few more hours as the kids frolicked in the water. Then she packed up and headed home. It was late and the kids were tired, so she hit the drive-through window on the way.

Drake was barely awake when Amber and the kids walked through the door. He smelled Chinese food. Annie ran through the living room and shouted, "Daddy, we won!"

"That's nice, honey, but try to keep it down. Daddy has a headache." His words were dry and unemotional, as he barely registered what his daughter had said. Annie lowered her head and walked away.

"You did great, sweetie. Daddy and I are super proud of you." She shot Drake a nasty glare.

Amber settled both kids at the table with dinner then turned to Drake. He sported an 'I'm sorry' look that wasn't quite convincing enough. Still, she handed him the carton of Mongolian beef.

He accepted it, but his wide eyes and hesitant movements showed he remained cautious. "Thanks."

Drake didn't remember much about the night before, but the soreness in his cheek warned him to choose his words carefully around Amber for the next few moments.

Occasionally, during dinner, Amber glanced over at him, and he rubbed at the few small welts on his face. She smiled and looked a little guilty, but satisfied.

When everyone finished dinner, Amber cleared the table, bathed both of the children, and put them to bed while Drake lay on the couch catching up on sports.

"You missed it again, Drake." His angry wife approached the couch out of the corner of his eye.

"Missed what?"

"Annie's soccer game. I realize you don't have time to coach anymore, but the least you could do is show up and cheer her on."

Drake rubbed his hands over his face for a moment in regret. "Why didn't you wake me up?"

"I tried, but you were dead to the world. … Sorry, poor choice of words."

He turned to make eye contact when Amber grabbed the remote and flicked the television off.

"We need to talk."

Drake recognized that tone in her voice. It reminded him of what he had done wrong.

"Okay, if this is about me forgetting our anniversary—"

"Again! … You forgot it again. Does our marriage, our relationship, not mean anything to you, Drake? Do *I* not mean anything to you?"

"Oh come on, give me a break!" His words were loud and abrasive. Amber pointed toward the kid's room and gestured a finger over her lips. Drake got the message and lowered his voice.

"I've got a lot on my mind, woman."

"And you think I don't? This happened to *both* of us in case you don't remember. I was there too. It was a terrible thing to go through, but we have two great kids who need us. You miss Annie's soccer games and have barely even hugged Max since that night." Amber bit her lip, and tears welled in her eyes. She brushed at them in an angry gesture.

Drake stood and grabbed his old Red Sox hat, then stormed out the door. Amber followed close behind and yelled, "You can't keep shutting me out! We have to deal with this!"

He cranked his truck and sped out of the driveway again. A few of the neighbors turned their porch lights on, so Amber stepped back inside and closed the door.

At that point, Max called out to his mom, obviously awoken from the noise. She went to him and stroked his soft, sandy blonde hair until he fell back to sleep.

Amber exited the bedroom, left the door ajar in case Max needed her again, and made her way to the couch. Gravity finally dominated and tears rolled down her cheeks without reservation. She wiped her eyes and spied a blue album that rested on the shelf of the entertainment center. A bookmark that featured the *Footsteps* poem allowed her to find the article with ease.

As Amber closed her eyes, she returned to *that night.* Only, she didn't see the flashing lights or hear the blaring sirens. Her mind always went back to the argument. The self-abusive thoughts took over once again:

If only I hadn't been so selfish. It was a great opportunity for Drake, and he had been so supportive of my career all those years. That night could have ended so much better. Maybe we would have come home and celebrated his promotion with an all-night love-making session. Instead, Drake disappeared to God knows where for a few days. I still wonder where he went.

Everything had been put into perspective for her after that fateful night. Amber realized that time with her children was borrowed, not promised, and she wanted to be there for every moment of their lives.

Drake, on the other hand, couldn't deal with the pain of what *he* had done, and took the complete opposite path. He buried himself in his work, and avoided Amber and the kids. Every time he walked out the door, Amber worried it was the last time she'd ever see him.

They once were best friends who did everything together, even before the kids came along. Why was he shutting her and the kids out? What had she done to make him not want to be with them?

For the first time in their lives together, Amber felt estranged to her husband. He was going through something even *she* couldn't help with.

Amber replaced the newspaper clipping back in the album with careful movements, and once again, she went to bed alone. As she rested her head on a tear-soaked pillow, she wondered where Drake had gone.

Chapter Five

That Night

Meanwhile, the bars had closed. Not ready to face Amber yet, Drake had called a *friend*.

"Hey babe, it's me. Feel like some company?"

A half-hour later, he lay in the arms of a beautiful leggy blonde with crystal blue eyes and peachy complexion. After what she could only consider meaningless, animal passion, the two lay side-by-side but barely touched.

"Feel better?" It was a rhetorical question. Gretchen had come to terms with the fact that she was nothing more than his *last call on a lonely night*, and actually felt sorry for him. He was dealing with some pretty powerful demons, but would never open up to her about them. She would never be *that* girl for him.

Drake turned to face the wall.

Gretchen always seemed to go for the love 'em and leave 'em type. After three failed marriages, no kids thankfully, she had not been in a serious relationship in years. The fact that Drake had a wife didn't make much of a difference. Her views on marriage were severely skewed when she found her first husband in bed with her sister.

Her motto had become, "Better to be the cheater than to be cheated on."

Drake barely even took notice when Gretchen softly slipped out of the bed. She flaunted her double-D mountains of perfection, and size twenty-four waistline, as she disappeared into the bathroom for a moment. When she reappeared, Drake was nowhere to be found.

"Surprise, surprise."

She turned the light off and went back to bed alone.

***

As he drove home, broken images from that fateful night flooded his mind. For a brief moment, the past morphed with the present—flashing lights, a sea of cops and paramedics, the whoosh of the chopper blades. He remembered looking over at Amber, as she comforted their screaming children.

"Ugh, get it together, Drake," he scolded himself.

He felt satisfied sexually, but completely empty everywhere else that mattered, so he headed home, and hoped Amber was asleep.

***

A little more sober than last time, Drake quietly pulled into the drive and killed the headlights. He slipped in the front door and sat on the couch for a moment to gather his thoughts. The blue album on the entertainment center drew his eyes. Once again, the bookmark led the way, and Drake opened it to the article with very little effort. Despite remembering the gory details all too well, he sat and read:

'Boy dies on way to emergency room after being struck by the vehicle of a local man and woman.'

A tear betrayed him as he continued to read:

'Local anchorwoman, Amber Woods, was in the passenger seat of the Honda SUV that struck a twelve-year-old boy as he tried to cross the street. Amber's husband Drake, was driving the vehicle at the time. Allegedly, the couple was in a heated argument, after an anniversary dinner they'd shared at a local bistro earlier that night. Authorities arrived on the scene just moments after the little boy was found. He was not breathing and lacked a pulse. Drake Woods administered CPR on the boy until emergency services arrived and took over. Little Deacon Smith was later pronounced dead at the Providence Medical Center on Friday, May 2, 2003. Authorities say the child was riding his bike to a friend's house in the dark without reflectors. No charges were filed against Mr. Woods or his wife. No comments have been made by either family at this time.'

Drake closed his eyes while his version of the events that preceded the incident played back in his mind, like an all-too-familiar, old song. How could they report it in such a callous way? ... So cold and unfeeling. Nothing like the emotional hell he was living in day in and day out.

Drake wiped his eyes, placed the article back inside the blue album, and returned it to the shelf. Then he made his way to his bed, as thoughts of regret filled his head. If given a chance, he would have done so many things differently.

Chapter Six

Two for the Show

Amber glanced down at her watch for the hundredth time; it looked as if he wasn't going to show. She had just left Annie backstage with the other cast members, and scanned the theatre for an empty seat near the front. Max was settled in the seat next to her. As he played a fish game on a muted iPad, Amber hoped it would keep him entertained long enough for her to at least see Annie's part.

Ms. Wilson, the music teacher at Annie's school, took the stage. She was a petite woman in her mid-forties with ash blonde, curly hair, and glasses. The Kindergarten class of Trinity Academy was putting on a production of *Little Red Riding Hood*, and Annie, the only red-haired girl in her class, had been given the role of Little Red. Amber scanned the entrance once more. Where was Drake?

"Welcome, parents. Your children are very excited to perform for you tonight. They have all been working hard to learn these parts. Please give them a round of applause and enjoy the show."

Just as her daughter took the stage, Amber heard Drake at the back entrance of the theatre.

"Hey, where's my wife? My daughter is the star tonight, you know."

Amber felt mortified. He was drunk again. She grabbed Max's hand, met her husband in the foyer, and escorted him to the parking lot.

"You're late, and hammered." She spoke softly and in code, as their son was close by.

"What are you doing, woman? I'm here to see our little girl in the play. Let's go." He slurred his words as he tried to push past her toward the entrance. Amber detested the way he issued that title, "*woman.*" He only assigned it to her when he was drunk.

"*You* are not going in there to embarrass me and our daughter. You can barely walk. Go sit in the truck and sleep off your buzz." Amber pointed toward his Silverado.

"I'm fine and I'm going to see my baby girl." Drake's voice boomed loud and angry.

He pushed Amber to the side, and made his way back into the theatre. He stumbled over the other parents with loud "excuse me's", and finally planted himself in an empty seat near the front. Amber and Max stayed toward the back to prevent more disturbances. The play was halfway over by that time.

When he saw his daughter on stage, he stood and yelled, "Hey baby, I'm here! Daddy's here!"

Annie forgot her lines for a moment, when she recognized her dad. She offered him a quick smile, and tried to get through her next few scenes. Amber sank low in her seat, completely humiliated for her daughter.

When the show was over, Amber looked over and saw Drake passed out in his seat. She wouldn't be able to wake him, so she left him there to sleep off his bad decisions. Then, she met Annie backstage with a congratulatory hug, and took both kids home.

***

About an hour later, a man awakened Drake when he shook his arm abruptly.

"Sir, sir. Are you okay? The show is over and you're going to have to leave. I need to close the building down for the night," the man informed him.

Drake felt groggy and his words were slurred as he inquired about his wife and kids.

"Sorry, sir. I don't know who you're talking about, but the theatre has been empty for about forty-five minutes. Do you need me to call you a cab?"

Drake got a good look at the man, an elderly African American gentleman. He wore a gray jumpsuit and had a broom in his left hand—obviously the janitor. Drake felt humiliated, apologized to the man, and he declined the cab offer. He made his way to his truck, and sat in the parking lot for a few more minutes to gather his composure, then headed home.

Amber pretended to be asleep. It had been a long, exhausting night, and she didn't have the energy for another argument. She cringed as she heard him fumble to get his key in the door. When he was able to open it, she felt a small hint of relief. At least he had sobered up enough to let himself in.

Drake made his way to the kitchen for a drink of water, brushed his teeth, and then climbed into bed. Within moments, his obnoxious snores began.

Amber sent a nod of gratitude to the Lord above for letting her avoid another fight with him, and for allowing her husband to make it home safely, once again.

Chapter Seven

Thank God for Yoga

Amber filled her friend in on all the horrific details of the previous night.

"Just leave the bastard." That was Janie's advice, as she went into the tree pose.

"It's not that simple. We have two kids together. He's not the father he once was, but I know he would not be okay with me taking the kids away from him." Amber mirrored her friend's stance.

"He humiliated you, and Annie. What kind of *father* does that?"

"I'm not even sure he realized it. When he came home last night, he didn't even bring it up. His drinking has really gotten bad."

"Well, I don't see how you put up with the skirting around. I wouldn't stand for that." Janie's southern drawl revealed itself once again.

Though she had always maintained a healthy respect for women with strong southern values, like Janie, Amber used to feel sorry for them, because of all the things they gave up in life, until *she* became one. The two women had a lot in common, and Amber treasured their friendship. Her deepest, darkest secrets were safe with Janie. Amber grew up without sisters, so she'd not had a relationship with another woman like that since college.

"Not like he's bringing anything home to me. We haven't had sex in months." Amber looked down at the floor. It was the first time she had actually uttered that truth aloud and was a bit ashamed of it.

"Whoa girl, you need some release. Why don't I take the kids for a while after class, and you go have a *lunch date* with Paul? He's got it bad for you, honey."

Both women laughed and fell out of position.

"Ladies, are we here to yoga or gossip?" Paul walked over, then directed wink at Amber. He then proceeded to reposition her body to the proper stance from behind.

Paul stood about five-eight with a muscular, athletic build and perfect abs. His sandy blonde hair and icy blue eyes made him the kind of guy one would expect to see on a GQ Magazine cover, but with a very down-to-earth persona, which made him even hotter to Amber. She was human, and of course found him very attractive, but knew she would never cheat on Drake. Though, it sure was fun to watch him flex his tight little bottom in the downward facing dog pose.

Paul had locked eyes with her a few times during the class, but she just shrugged it off as harmless flirting. Plus, other than those few fleeting moments, Paul had never given her a reason to believe he was interested in anything more than a class fee. She felt his eyes on her, as she flexed into compromising positions, but she considered it the same reaction any other hot-blooded male would have displayed.

Besides, no one could have overlooked the huge diamond wedding ring on her finger, which screamed TAKEN. Nerves all jittery, she felt the back of the band with her left thumb for a moment.

Amber adored her wedding ring set. Though she still hadn't gotten that dream wedding, Drake did take his first big pay check in New York and buy her a gorgeous, custom-designed, one carat, princess-cut diamond ring, with a luster that put the stars to shame.

Guess life doesn't always have a fairytale ending. Truth be told, she would have given anything to have her original ring set back, if it meant she could have her old life back too.

Before they knew it, class was over and the ladies headed to the gym child care center to collect their children.

Chapter Eight

The Apology

Monday morning came a little too soon and yet not soon enough for Drake. The events of his weekend had left him tired, but he sought refuge from the wrath of Amber back in his office in the city.

New York was a great place to be in the spring. The city was alive with street performers and deafening sirens—distractions which someone who wanted to drown out their own self-defeating thoughts might welcome.

Drake reached his desk to find a smorgasbord of pink and yellow post-its about upcoming business meetings and deadlines. He usually dreaded those things, but they were welcome distractions from his home life at that moment. As he peeled them off one by one, a particular note caught his attention— 'Don't forget about your anniversary, Karen.'

He glanced at the photos on his desk. Annie was just a toddler when they last had family portraits taken. Had it really been that long? He ran his fingers gently over their faces, and then his eyes shifted to a picture of Amber. She held both kids in her lap and smiled as if the sun itself lived inside her mouth.

If only he hadn't been so selfish when Amber wanted to take that job in Seattle. The New York job hadn't turned out to be as good as he had imagined it. Between the late hours and long commute, he dragged his feet through the doorway after dark during the week, and slept most of his weekends away. Truth be told, he often wished he had just stayed in Kansas. At least he was with his kids more often there. Drake silently longed for the days when his life was simple—and perfectly chaotic.

A sweet female voice interrupted his thoughts. "Excuse me, Mr. Woods. Mr. Shelton would like to see you in his office." He looked up to see his assistant. "Let him know I'm on my way, Karen, thanks."

An all-business type of guy, Mr. Shelton had never married, he just had a multitude of girlfriends over the years. Not that Drake ever had much trouble with women, but that man had gorgeous women stuck to him like velcro, all the time. Drake concluded that it was the money. The man stood barely five-nine, weighed about two-hundred and fifty pounds, and had less hair on his head than most men had on one arm. But he did have exquisite taste. He drove a Maserati, and lived in a house with fifteen bathrooms (or at least that's how many Drake counted at the company Christmas party). He wore expensive Italian suits, and had a bottle of 1858 Croizet Cuvee Leonie, (worth more than one-hundred and fifty thousand dollars), sitting in his office at all times. Ironically, Drake had never seen the man drink a drop of it. That was how Mr. Shelton rolled. He liked to own expensive things, even if he didn't need them; a lifestyle that intrigued

Drake but terrified him at the same time. He sat there for what seemed like an eternity. Sweat coated his palms and he dreaded the coming conversation. After he checked several emails and made a few notes at his desk, Mr. Shelton finally spoke:

"Drake, you're falling down on the job. Your last two drafts were a mess, and you missed two lunch dates with major potential clients. I spent a lot of time and money to get you here because I heard you were the best man for the job, but so far I haven't seen much of a return on my investment."

Before Drake could answer to his recent lack of performance, Mr. Shelton continued, "I am placing you on probation for thirty days. If I don't see some significant changes soon, I'm going to have to let you go. Many architects would kill for this job."

Drake acknowledged his shortcomings, and promised to make amends right away. Then Mr. Shelton excused him. He cursed himself all the distance back to his office. When he reached his desk, he made a few apologetic phone calls to clients, reset some meetings, finished several drawings, and before he knew it, the day was over. He hadn't even stopped for lunch.

Drake locked his office door and headed home, but not before he stopped by the florist. What type of flower would say, 'Sorry I missed our anniversary, again'?

***

For the first time in a few months, he had made it home before dark. Amber was clearing the dinner dishes and the kids were getting ready for bed. She gave Drake a forced smile when he walked through the door and sat the flowers on the table. She wasn't really surprised he was home early, since that had been his pattern for the past few years. Once the alcohol wore off, and he came back to reality a few days later, Drake would always bring her flowers and apologize for "the whole anniversary thing," as he called it. Amber was tired of his apologies and excuses. Although she was a strong woman, there's only so much a person can take. It was time for an ultimatum.

Drake played the apologetic husband role to the end that night. He put the kids to bed while Amber wrapped up in the kitchen. They said prayers together and Drake returned to the kitchen to find his dinner plate in the microwave.

As he sat to eat, Amber positioned herself across the table from him and said, "We need to talk."

Drake didn't blow up at her like before. He kept his mouth shut and listened.

"I can't keep living like this. You are rarely home anymore, and when you are, you're either drunk or passed out from exhaustion. The kids deserve better, I deserve better! This is not what I signed up for."

Drake interrupted. "I know. I'm going to make it better. I promise. Just give me time."

"You're running out of time, Drake. Your kids are growing up without you. Before you know it, they'll be moving away and you'll be wishing you had this time back. This job has consumed you and we are no longer a priority for you."

"So, what are you saying, Amber? You want a divorce or something? You want me to quit my job? I have to work. Someone has to bring in a pay check around here." His words were cold and harsh, and apparently he had conveniently forgotten that it was a joint decision for Amber to be a stay-home mom, when he took the job in New York.

Money wasn't the real issue. They both knew that, but both continued to stand their positions.

"I don't want a divorce. I want you to stand up for yourself at work and demand a better schedule, to allow you to be home with us more." Amber wiped soft streams from her eyes, and tried to regain her composure.

"You know I can't do that. Mr. Shelton depends on me. I'm head of the team."

"Then I guess you've made your decision." Amber stood with her arms folded, which signified there was no compromise to be made in that moment.

"Look, we're both angry and still sore about the weekend. Let's just get some sleep and talk about this in the morning, okay? I have a big day tomorrow."

Drake pulled in close to attempt a kiss, only to be met with Amber's cheek. Their argument wasn't going to end the way she wanted, so she agreed—with reluctance—to let it go for the night. They faced opposite directions, and made sure not to touch throughout the night.

Bedtime was once the favorite part of both of their days. Their bodies practically melted in to one, and their limbs remained intertwined for the duration of the night. It seemed as if they weren't able to get close enough at times.

But over time, a wall had been built between them, and a distance separated them. It seemed nothing could take it away, not even their love.

Chapter Nine

The Proposition

After the heated conversation the night before, Amber very much looked forward to releasing some stress in yoga class this morning. Unfortunately, Janie was home nursing her daughter back to health, due to a cold, and Amber had to fly solo.

She could almost feel the stress seeping out through every pore in her body, as she breathed deeply, and stretched out her muscles. Without Janie there, as much as she missed her friend's company, she was able to focus on each move completely.

Amber thought she noticed Paul deliberately make eye contact a few times. He probably wondered where Janie was.

***

After class finished, and the room had cleared, Paul seized the opportunity to find Amber without her sidekick, for once, and made his way over to strike up a conversation.

"Looking good, Amber; you are really flexible. I'm amazed at the progress you've made in my class." He touched her shoulder lightly, but it was enough to send chills through her spine—in a good way.

She took a breath and tried to sound casual. "Well, I have a great teacher." Amber distanced herself from him. She tried to appear distracted as she gathered her belongings.

He was close enough for Amber to get a good whiff of his manly essence. Even dripping with sweat, he smelled delicious somehow. Paul wasn't one of those male instructors who wore Speedos and cheesy sweat bands. He sported a white wife-beater, with a pair of black, loose-legged yoga pants that clung to every muscle in his body, not in an offensive way, but just tight enough to showcase his *attributes*.

"I'd love to give you some *private* lessons in flexibility sometime if you're interested." Paul traced up and down her arm with his soft fingers. Amber finally realized he was making a move on her. It had been a long time since any man had looked at her that way, much less touched her that sensually. It was the kind of attention she used to get from Drake.

Afraid that he might hear her heart pounding as loudly as she felt it, Amber backed up a bit and flashed her ring.

"I'm married, Paul." She turned around to pick up her purse, and hoped to hide her crimson face.

She felt the heat expel through her pores, like invisible waves that hovered over an asphalt turf mid-summer. He aroused feelings in her that had been pushed below the surface for a long time.

"Happily?" he inquired, as he moved closer behind. She felt his breath on her neck. His hands traced her hips slowly, in quest of every curve he could find, as he whispered tantalizing sentiments in her ear.

"I've heard you and Janie talking about that husband of yours. He's a fool for not realizing what a treasure he has. I can treat you so much better, like the queen you are." His hands were slow and deliberate. "A body this hot should be worshiped not ignored."

Amber hadn't heard words like that in a very, very long time. Her heart raced. It felt nice to be wanted again. His hands were velvet on her skin. Still, she pushed him off—though a little delayed, she was ashamed to admit to herself.

She backed away and stumbled over the bench as she stammered. "I-I gotta go get my kids. Th-thanks for a great class." Then she made her way to the gym child-care area, collected her children, and walked to the car.

As she drove, she couldn't stop smiling. Amber didn't care if she caught cold; she *had* to tell Janie what had happened.

***

"Oh my God!" Janie let out a scream, and then quickly muffled it, with a cupped hand over her mouth. The two women sat on Janie's bed to talk, which was within earshot of where her sick daughter rested.

"I know! I didn't know how to react, so I got out of there as fast as possible, but not before I made a complete fool of myself. I tripped over my words ... and the bench." She lifted her pants leg to show Janie the red mark on her shin.

"Girl, you should have gone for it. I told you I would watch the kids."

"I can't. I'm married. That would make me no better than Drake if I did." Amber resented that truth, especially after her husband had all but confessed that he had cheated on her just a few nights before.

Janie probed for more details. "Did he smell delicious?"

Amber barely allowed her friend to finish her question. "How can a man have such an alluring scent after a workout like that? It's like sweat mixed with vanilla or something." Both women burst out laughing.

"It's called pheromones, honey. It's the come hither scent that exists when a man and woman are attracted to one another." Janie smiled and winked at her friend.

"You know, we have to find another yoga place now. I can't show my face there again. I would be mortified. Besides, now that I know how he feels about me, I won't be able to focus."

Janie sighed and stuck out her lip. The two women talked for a little while longer, then Janie's daughter awoke from her nap, and called out for *mommy*. Amber could see that Janie really wanted to stay and hear more details about her friend and the 'hot yoga guy', but her motherly duties always took precedence.

Amber gave her an easy out. "It's getting late. I've got to go feed the kids. Call you later."

They exchanged hugs, and Amber loaded her kids into the car. She wanted to get them to bed at a decent hour, so she grabbed two Happy Meals on the way home.

As soon as they walked through the door, she gave them dinner and put them to bed. Then, she locked herself in the bathroom for a private moment … and a cold shower.

***

As usual, Drake came in after Amber had gone to bed, though she only pretended to be asleep. Without so much as even a goodnight kiss from her husband, she lay in bed thinking about all the events that had transpired that day. She caressed her neck and ran her fingers down the length of her arm as she thought about how Paul had done the same just hours before.

Her mind wrestled with her heart about what she needed to do, versus what she *wanted* to do. She hadn't known Paul very long, and wasn't even certain she had real feelings for him—well not the loving kind anyway. It was more of an animal hunger that made her mouth water. She licked her lips, like a dog vying for a morsel of steak to be dropped to the floor during dinner. Oh God. Had it really been that long since she'd had sex?

It wasn't like her to have lustful thoughts about other men. Drake was the only man she desired, but she couldn't remember the last time he made her feel as wanted as Paul did. Amber finally slowed her mind, and drifted off to sleep. Scattered images of her kids, and the life she'd built with Drake, played out like an 8mm motion film. One in which Paul had begun to make frequent appearances.

Chapter Ten

The Best Laid Plans

The alarm sounded for the umpteenth time. Drake darted out of bed and dressed furiously. He would be late, and that wouldn't look good for his first day of probation, which he hadn't yet mentioned to Amber.

Drake kissed his kids on the forehead, and stroked his wife's hair with a soft touch. As she slept, his eyes lingered on her face, almost as if he might never see her again. Then he grabbed his keys and headed to work.

***

Amber waited for him to pull out of the drive before she got up to dress. Coupled with the events that had transpired with Paul, and the inappropriate dream she had just awoken from, Amber knew what had to be done.

She figured on at least ten hours, maybe more with traffic, to get some things done. Her plan was to have as much as possible packed before the kids awoke.

Amber worked efficiently as she sifted through the closet she shared with Drake. Occasionally, her momentum was slowed when she caught a whiff of his natural scent on one of his shirts. Not all of them reeked of his indiscretions with other women.

She pressed her face to it, closed her eyes, and breathed in the memories. Once it had taken all the self-control she could muster, to not rip his shirt off and slather his chest with kisses every time their eyes met.

Amber let out a deep, longing sigh. It would never be like that again, and she had to do what was right for her and the kids. What would he say, or do, when he realized they were gone? No matter, she wasn't changing her mind.

Her thoughts were soon interrupted by the pitter-patter of little feet, and cereal boxes being ripped open, so she made her way into the kitchen to greet the children.

"Good morning, sleepyheads. Are you guys ready for a road trip today?"

The kids sat at the table with sleep-filled eyes, as they barely chewed their cereal. Amber studied their little faces, and wondered how Drake didn't want to be with them every minute possible. He used to be addicted to the kids. Everything the Woods did, they did as a family. In fact, Amber was often jealous of the time he spent with them over alone time with her.

Suddenly, she realized that she had just described Janie and Brad's relationship—almost platonic. Perhaps that was where everything went wrong? Wow, she and Janie had more in common than she'd thought. Amber sighed when she realized how much she was going to miss her friend.

When breakfast was over, the kitchen cleaned, and everything was put away, she sent the kids to their rooms to gather some things for the trip, as she headed back to hers. She had already done all the laundry for the week, which made it easier.

Just an hour later, everything was done. She could send for the rest later, if needed. The plan was just to go away for a few days to clear her head anyway.

All the electric items were turned off. Amber laid a folded letter across his pillow, with only the word 'Drake' written on it. She took one long look around and closed the door behind her.

***

Janie's daughter felt much better, so Amber and the kids stopped by for one last play date, though she hadn't told her friend that part yet. They took the kids to the park. Amber thought it might be easier to break away publicly, rather than in the comfort of her best friend's backyard, where so many wonderful memories could easily be recounted. She had come too far to have her emotions cause a change of heart.

As the children cascaded down the slide, and reveled in the back and forth motion of the swings, Amber broke the news to her friend.

"I'm gonna miss you so much, girl." Janie's southern drawl really came out when she was emotional about something.

"I know; me too. But you were right. I can't keep doing this to myself, and the kids. We deserve better. And it's not permanent. I just need to take a break for a while and gather my thoughts." Amber grabbed her friend's hand.

"I'll call you when we're halfway there. If you don't hear from me, it just means my cell phone battery died or something. Whatever you do, don't tell Drake about this if he calls you. I want to get settled, and make sure the kids are distracted when we have that conversation. I don't want him to call me on the road."

Janie promised to keep her friend's secret, and the two women held each other for a few minutes more, and watched the kids play. Before parting ways, Amber handed her friend a piece of paper.

"This is the address. Write me and call a lot, okay?" Tears filled her eyes.

Both women hugged, and then Amber set out for the interstate. She hoped the kids would sleep most of the way.

***

Drake sat patiently in traffic, and listened to the radio. An unfinished conversation awaited him at home, and he was not looking forward to it. Despite the fact that his day had begun late and rushed, he had actually managed to get to the office on time and experienced quite a productive day. As he flipped through the radio stations, a woman's soft, empathetic voice invaded the airways:

"I-70 has been closed down tonight until further notice due to a recent head on collision between a Honda SUV and a Ford F250 Duramax truck. All drivers and passengers, including a woman and two children, have been Life Flighted to St. Mary's Trauma Center. No word on their condition as of yet. Stay tuned to WSB to bring you breaking news as this story develops."

Drake heard stories of that nature all the time on his commute. He shook his head, and released a sigh of sympathy for those involved, then continued flipping through. Finally, he decided to jam out to rock songs from the Eighties. As those heart-wrenching ballads filled the atmosphere of his truck, he felt a little more confident and optimistic about the conversation he was going to have with Amber. He imagined it would end with their limbs entangled, close enough to feel the blood pulse through each other's veins. The thought of that brought a devilish smile to his face. Something told him a great night lay ahead.

When Drake pulled in the driveway, he thought it odd to not see Amber's car there. She must have stopped off at Janie's after yoga. That gave him plenty of time.

He worked quickly as he entered the door, and didn't even stop to put his coat away. Drake checked the microwave and stove, and found that Amber had not yet made dinner. There wasn't enough time to cook, so he called around to a local bistro, and ordered a juicy rack of lamb with baby red potatoes, two Caesar salads, fresh brochette, and even cheesecake for dessert. Then he dialed the local 24-hour florist, and ordered three dozen purple roses. (After all, in New York City, you could have a bulldozer delivered to your door at 3am if you tried hard enough). He took down two wine glasses and a bucket to fill with ice cubes. Drake dusted off the bottle of Dom Perignon his boss had given to the couple when they had first arrived.

He found a CD and placed it in the player. A sweet, soulful voice wailed out a heartbreaking tune— something about loving someone too long to stop now. Then he sprinkled soft, purple rose petals throughout the living room, hallway, and all over the kitchen table. When it was all done, Drake stood back and admired his handiwork. Perfect.

Two hours later, the food had been delivered and had gone cold. It sat on the exquisitely garnished table untouched. Drake glanced at the clock and realized just how late it was. The big ball of fire in the sky had sunken behind the trees, and not even a trace of horizon remained visible.

He tried to call her cell a few times, as he continued to look out the window, but it went straight to voicemail each time.

"Dammit. She always forgets to charge her phone before she goes out." His voice sounded angry and frustrated. It hadn't been quite long enough to garner concern from him.

Drake left another, that time testy, voicemail. Then he walked toward the bathroom in pursuit of a shower, while he waited. As he sifted through the closet, he didn't even notice that most of her clothes were missing. But when he walked by the bed, his eyes caught a glimpse of a neatly folded paper on the pillow. His heart sank into his stomach, in fear of what it meant. He read:

Dear Drake,

I'm sorry it has come to this for us. I want you to know that I have loved you from the moment we first met in that diner, though I was too proud to show it.

I tried to have it all—the career, and being a good mom and wife. You were the best father I could have ever chosen for our children, in the beginning. But lately it seems we are more of an inconvenience than a priority for you, so we are going somewhere we will be loved and appreciated. I will call you when we get there, but please give us some space for now. I need time to figure some things out and clear my head. The kids are safe, and we will call you when we arrive.

I will always love you, but I love myself and the kids too much to keep living this way. Talk with you soon.

Amber

When he finished reading, his head dropped into his hands. Tears flowed down his face like tiny rivers in pursuit of the ocean. What had he done? Why did he wait so long? Soon, anger overcame him and the questions changed. Who the hell did she think she was, taking his kids away? How dare she?

He dried his face, gathered his composure, and tried her cell a few more times. With still no luck, he began to make other phone calls. Janie was the first person to enter his mind.

Amber's friend played her part, just as she had been instructed. "Sorry, I haven't seen or heard from her today, Drake."

Drake thanked Janie and sat quietly for a few minutes, as he tried to think of anyone else he could call. He soon realized that Amber didn't have many friends, or at least he didn't know who they were. It hit him just how disconnected he had become with his wife. After he called the last local person he could think of, to no avail, he dialed Jill's number.

Chapter Eleven

Mother-in-Law

Jill remained leery of her son-in-law—especially after the emotional conversations she and Amber had shared recently. Of course, no one would ever be good enough for her daughter, in her mind.

Only this time, when he called, there was an apparent concern in her voice, one he had never heard before.

"Hello?" Jill's voice was broken and frantic. "Amber is that you?"

"Hello, Jill. No, it's me, Drake. What's wrong? Have you heard from Amber?"

"Oh, Drake. No, I haven't. She was supposed to call me when she had made it halfway here." Jill was so worried, that she forgot to keep her daughter's secret.

Drake was furious. "What do you mean, here? There in Kansas with you?"

"We can talk about this later. Right now we need to find her. I've been calling her for hours now and no answer. I'm worried."

"Okay, stay by the phone. I'm going out to look for her. Call me if you hear from her first. You have my cell number?"

"Yes, yes I have it. I will … and Drake, please call me the minute you find out something."

"I promise." He tried not to imagine the worst.

***

The conversation ended, and he searched for his keys, with no clue as to where to start looking. *Oh God—she was on the way to her mother's house. She would have gotten on I-70 near Virginia to head to Kansas.* The phone fell from his hand.

Finally, he found the keys and ran to his truck in a fever. Immediately, he turned the station back to WSB, and headed toward I-70. He hoped that he would find her car broken down on the side of the road. A dead cell phone or stalled engine was much easier to think about than the alternative. As he drove, the announcer came over the airwaves with, *"Breaking news on the I-70 accident from earlier this evening."* Drake turned it up.

"Around 5:30 this evening, a woman and her two children were riding along I-70, when a black Ford F250 hit them head on. The driver of the truck was allegedly under the influence. He has been released from St. Mary's Trauma Center with minimal injuries and was immediately transferred to the county jail. He is being held without bail for drunken driving, with possible additional charges pending. The woman and two children are still in critical condition, and have not yet been identified. We will continue to bring you live updates as this story develops. Thank you for choosing …"

Drake turned off the radio. He sobbed and his body shook. With no time to waste, he grabbed his cell phone and dialed information.

A woman's voice came over the line. "What listing would you like?"

"St. Mary's Trauma Center." His words came out faint with utter disbelief.

A few moments later, another woman's voice spoke.

"St. Mary's Trauma Center, how may I help you?"

"Yes, do you have an Amber Woods admitted there?" He hoped the answer was no.

"Are you family, sir?" the lady asked politely and slowly.

"Yes, I'm … I'm her husband."

Husband, wow, he hadn't really lived up to that title in a while. What kind of husband cheated on his wife, blamed her for his inability to control his demons, and practically pushed her into the hands of death? A shitty one for sure.

"Sir, sir? Are you still there?"

His mind returned to the moment. "Yes, I'm here."

"Okay, sir, I need you to come to the hospital and speak to the doctor personally. There are a few documents you will need to sign. Do you have our address?"

Drake told her he did, and assured the lady that he was on his way. It was only about an hour's drive, but he was determined to make it in thirty minutes or less. He wasn't concerned about getting a ticket, or possibly sending *himself* to that hospital in a helicopter. For the first time in quite a while, all he could think about was getting to his wife and kids.

It would be best not to call Amber's mother until he spoke to the doctor, and knew all the details … and the projected outcome.

All the way to the hospital, Drake did something he had not done in quite some time—he prayed.

Chapter Twelve

Dr. *Who?*

Drake didn't remember if he had stopped at traffic lights or stop signs along the way. He barely had the patience for the automated glass doors, as he burst into to the hospital. An elderly woman greeted him at the front desk. She had graying hair, a few wrinkles around her eyes, covered with glasses that sat comfortably on the bridge of her nose, and sported a lipstick color that for sure went out of fashion in the Eighties.

She obviously had experience with many panic-stricken loved ones, and took control of the situation immediately. Her voice was soft and understanding, as she tried to stop him from breaking down the entrance doors to the triage area.

"Excuse me, sir. What is the patient's name?"

Her mellow voice felt comforting, and his breath slowed long enough for him to say, "My, my wife. I'm looking for my wife. Her name is Amber, Amber Woods." His words sounded broken.

Normally, Drake spoke in an eloquent manner. Many of his co-workers referred to him as 'Lord of the living room.' But in that moment, he couldn't find that voice.

"Okay, Mr. Woods. Please have a seat for just a moment and I will locate your wife, if she is here."

Drake barely sat on the edge of a seat nearest the reception desk. His hands shook and he realized he had not eaten since lunch, because he had been waiting for Amber to join him at the lovely dinner table he had prepared. What if he was too late? He vowed to always protect her and the kids, but had let them all down more than once.

The nurse's soft voice interrupted his self-abusive thoughts. "Mr. Woods. I've found your wife and children. I am going to let you through these doors now, if you promise me you will calm down and won't upset the staff on the other side." She had a grandmotherly tone to her voice that let him know she was kind, but serious.

"Yes, of course."

She could tell that Drake was trying to prove he was now in control of his emotions.

"Okay, sir. Once you go through these double doors, you will see a small waiting room about three doors down. Please have a seat there, and the doctor will come fill you in. He is expecting you. Take these papers and fill them out while you wait."

Drake's feet tore a cautious but swift path to the double doors, and stopped when he reached the waiting room. His hands trembled as he filled out the papers. Then, he alternated between sitting and standing, unable to settle, as he anticipated the doctor's arrival. After what seemed like an eternity,

Drake spied a white coat out of the corner of his eye.

"Mr. Woods?" A deep, soothing voice summoned him.

Drake turned to see a male physician, possibly in his late fifties, who sported a head full of dark black hair, and appeared to be in excellent physical shape. He shook the doctor's hand as he confirmed his name.

"I am Dr. Davis. I am the surgeon on your wife's case. We need to talk about your wife's current condition." His words were spoken in a matter-of-fact tone, almost with arrogance.

Drake sat down. The words "We need to talk," echoed in his mind. He had heard those words from Amber many times, especially lately, and good news never followed.

"Is she alive?" He could barely summon his voice to ask the question.

"She is, but remains in critical condition. Amber suffered severe trauma to the head and is currently in a coma. Amazingly, she came through with only a few broken bones, and those can be mended. Our major concern right now is her brain. We were able to stop the hemorrhaging, but there is still quite a bit of swelling left behind. We are monitoring that now and giving her ..."

Drake's head felt as though it had swelled. His ears rang. He wanted to hear every word the doctor said, but his heart pounded louder than the doctor's voice, and his tears masked his sight. He pictured his sweet love lying on a hospital bed, hooked up to a plethora of machines and IV drips, as she clung to her last breath of life. He worried about the children too, but felt a powerful obligatory presence with the love of his life in that moment. After all, she was the reason he even became a father. *Where have these loving thoughts about her been hiding for so long?*

When Drake's mind and ears returned to the conversation, the doctor said, "I need to get back to check on Amber now. I will send the Chaplain in to speak with you. Is there anyone else you'd like us to call? Do you have any other questions for me?"

Drake only had one: "What now?"

"Now, we wait."

Chaplain. Drake knew what that meant. They only sent the Chaplain when the situation was dire, and when they thought he or she might need to get close enough to the family to support them ... in the end. Drake couldn't let his mind go there yet. He inquired about his children, as he offered their names.

***

Drake went to visit Max first. He was awake in the bed and watching *Scooby Doo*.

"Hey, Buddy." His dad handed him the stuffed dinosaur he had bought at the gift shop. "How are you feeling?" Drake longed to embrace his boy with every ounce of energy he had, but he knew to approach him carefully and gently for a while.

"Daddy!" the little boy squealed with joy when he saw his father's face.

Max had a big bandage across the left side of his head. Drake swallowed hard and tried to fight the tears in his eyes, but they betrayed him.

Another white coat appeared out of nowhere and said in soft tones, "This little guy was a trooper. Barely a bump or bruise to speak of. He is one tough boy." Even more quietly, so only Drake could hear, she added, "It was a miracle."

The woman that stood before him had long chestnut locks, which barely reached the tops of her breasts. She probably did yoga, like Amber. Her body was very thin and fit. Normally, Drake would have made an inappropriate advance or comment toward her, but his only focus, for once, was his family, and he barely made eye contact.

"I'm Doctor Leven. I was assigned to your son's case this evening."

Drake shook her hand half-heartedly, but hoped it was enough to show his gratitude. Then, he returned his eyes to Max, and stroked his hair.

"And my daughter?" His voice sounded nervous and relieved simultaneously.

"I think she was assigned to Dr. Ellis. I will go check on her status, and let you know where to find her." Dr. Leven disappeared just as quickly as she had come.

Drake sat with Max, and tried to stay patient while he awaited news on his wife and daughter. In his heart, he continued to pray.

"Daddy, we saw a big truck, and it hit us right in front of Mommy. Is Mommy okay?" Max had explained the accident so matter-of-factly, and with vivid description. Drake was amazed at how much his son's vocabulary had advanced. Still, he didn't want to upset Max with too many details.

"Mommy has some boo-boos, Buddy, but the doctors are taking really good care of her." Drake hoped he was right.

Moments later, Dr. Leven reappeared and informed Drake that Annie would be out of surgery soon, and that Dr. Ellis would come find him.

"Surgery?"

"She had a few lacerations on her stomach, apparently from the car seat, but no other serious injuries. She will be moved to a recovery room soon." Dr. Leven's voice was calm and assuring.

Again Drake sighed with relief. Both of his children were okay. He gave a thankful nod to the higher power above, and held his son for what seemed like an eternity, before another doctor came in.

A hand was extended to Drake and he took it, with a renewed strength, due to the recent news about his children.

The doctor was a male with short, spiked hair. The guy looked young enough to have just graduated from med school. *Is he really qualified to take care of my baby girl?*

"I'm Dr. Ellis. I am the surgeon assigned to Annie's case. She came through just fine and is in recovery now. You should be able to go see her momentarily. Do you have any questions for me, sir?"

Sir? He knew that the young doctor was being polite and professional, but hearing that word made Drake feel as if he'd aged ten years in that moment. Where had the years gone and why hadn't he treasured them more?

"No, Doctor, and thanks for letting me know. I appreciate you taking care of my little girl."

"Just doing my job, sir," the doctor replied with a smile. "You're a very lucky man, Mr. Woods."

Drake thought for a minute on that word, *lucky*. He had to agree, although he was convinced that *blessed* was a more suitable description. He prayed God would grant him one last favor.

Max was soon back to sleep, and Drake slipped out of the room to make some phone calls.

Chapter Thirteen

The Women in his Life

How could Drake break the news that Jill's little girl was in critical condition and fighting for her life? It would just reconfirm the previous suspicions she had of him—that he was too concerned about his own needs to make sure his family was taken care of. If it weren't for him, Amber never would have been on that road.

"Hi, Jill, it's me." He struggled to relocate the calm voice he had practiced. Drake took a deep breath and offered the good news first.

"The kids are both fine. I haven't seen Annie yet, but the doctor said she had only a few minor injuries."

"Oh thank you Jesus. And what about my Amber? Is she okay?" Broken breaths laced her voice.

Drake was quiet for a moment, perhaps a little too long. His ability to speak came and went in sporadic rhythms as he explained to Jill that her only daughter was holding on by a thread.

When he finished, she said something he didn't expect. "Well, I'm glad you are there with them, Drake. I know you love Amber and the kids."

Drake almost dropped the phone in shock. He had never experienced anything close to that level of support from her. As he thought about his recent excursions and bad choices, he felt ashamed and undeserving of her respect. But that was not the time or place to unburden his demons on anyone else, least of all the only person in the world who possibly loved Amber more than him.

After he hung up with Jill, Drake took a few moments to gather his thoughts, and then called his boss to inform him of the situation. To his surprise and relief, his boss was sympathetic, and said everything at the office would still be there when he returned.

Just as he hung up the phone, the young Dr. Ellis touched Drake lightly on the arm.

"Sorry to interrupt, Mr. Woods, but Annie is awake and asking for her Mom."

He put the phone back in his pocket, regained his height, and walked toward Annie's room.

***

"Hi, sweetheart, I heard you were quite the fighter today. That's my strong girl." He stroked the top of her hand gently. "I'm so proud of you."

Annie slowly turned her head toward her dad and said, "One minute mommy was crying and flipping through the radio, then a truck hit us out of nowhere and mommy was bleeding. Is she okay?"

Again, Drake felt flabbergasted at how much his daughter had matured recently. Her confidence reminded him a lot of her mother. A few tears escaped, but he erased them with his fingers.

"The doctors are working on her, sweetheart, but don't you worry. They are very good at their jobs." He was trying to convince himself with those words more than anyone else.

Dr. Ellis reappeared in the doorway. "Hi, Annie. You were a very brave and cooperative little girl today."

Annie was the analytical type. She asked about the machines that surrounded her, and the numerous medicines they had administered for pain.

"Wow, sounds like we might have a doctor on our hands here one day. Come find me when you are ready for a job, young lady."

Annie smiled, and then held her head for a moment.

"She has been complaining about a slight headache, but that could be from the stress of the situation. Although we didn't notice any trauma during the operation, we'd like to keep her for a couple of days for observation just in case."

Drake agreed, but somehow he knew his children were going to be okay, and hoped the same for their mother. He had already decided, in his heart, that things would be different from that day forward, but he certainly had no plans to be a single dad.

Annie sat up in the bed and asked questions about her brother and mother. Drake answered them all as honestly as he could. Once the doctors gave clearance, he wheeled Annie down to her brother's room so the three could be together. Later that evening, the hospital arranged for the siblings to have a family suite so they could unite more comfortably during their difficult situation. No news on Amber yet.

Chapter Fourteen

The Past is Not Always Left in the Past

Drake awoke the next morning with a stiff neck and his legs tingled from sleeping on the fold-out couch. But when he looked over at his two children sound asleep, the pain melted away, and a sweet breeze of peace replaced it.

Moments later, a news reporter and three camera crewmen invaded the room.

"Mr. Woods, I'm Sarah Malcom from Channel 6 Live News. Can you tell us how you are feeling after this terrible tragedy?"

A beautiful woman with straight, mid-length, chestnut-colored hair stood before him. She wore a royal blue skirt suit, white blouse, and nude heels, paired with flawless makeup. The reporter didn't wait for an answer.

"Can you update us on your wife's condition? Where were you when the accident occurred? Aren't you the couple from Kansas who hit the little boy?"

Drake was overwhelmed and a little groggy. For a second, his mind flashed back to the scene in Kansas. The flashing cameras, and reporters in his face asking questions he wasn't sure how—and didn't want—to answer.

Before he could respond, the hospital staff came in and cleared the room.

"No reporters allowed in this area. Get out or I'm calling security."

Drake thanked the nurse with a subtle nod, and moved over to comfort his children, who had been awakened by the intrusion.

***

While the kids ate lunch, Drake slipped out the door to inquire about his wife's condition. The doctors offered him the "no changes" response he had come to loathe, and then led him to her room.

She slept peacefully, with an abundance of beeping robotics all around her bed. The swelling had reduced, and she somewhat resembled his wife again. The doctors had let him briefly visit her the night before, but he was rushed out of the room when the nurses came in to run more tests, and informed him that his children were asking for him.

Drake walked over to her bed, and brushed the top of her hand, just as he had done with Annie. He hadn't noticed how beautiful she was lately. Despite the bruises, he could tell that her skin had been scarcely touched by the sun, but in a good way. Time had been good to her, even after two kids, and all the hell he had put her through. Drake pulled a chair close to her bed and held her hand. Then he lowered his head, seemingly in prayer, but in that moment, his words were for Amber.

"Baby, I'm so sorry I've let you down. I haven't been there for you and the kids, and I know that now. If it weren't for me, you wouldn't have had to run to your mother's house. I promised you I'd take care of you, and you'd never have to worry about anything. Turns out, I was the only one you *couldn't* count on."

He paused for a moment and tried to summon his voice again.

"I want to tell you something about *that night*. When we were fighting, I was so angry and focused on what I wanted, I completely discounted your feelings. Resentment took over me, and I almost, for a second, said that I wished I'd never even gotten married so young, because then I could chase my dreams."

His tears flowed uncontrollably, and he buried his shame in the bed sheet, unable to even look at her.

When he found his composure again, he continued, "I don't even know what came over me. I didn't mean it. It was just a passing selfish thought. But after the accident, I blamed myself … for feeling that way, and because my selfish actions took that little boy's life. I felt like I didn't deserve a family anymore. Every time I looked at Max, I thought of how I took a son away from his family. I just wanted to disappear. Our kids were better off with no father at all than one like me. I knew they were safe with you ..."

He lost it again, as he thought about how he wasn't able to protect his family from that horrible accident.

"Just please come back to me and the kids. I promise I will make every moment of our life together the fairytale you deserve. I'm so sorry, Amber. Please wake up and tell me you forgive me."

There was no response. After a few more moments in silence at her bedside, Drake returned to his children.

***

Three days later, the hospital released both children and they went to Grandma Jill's, while Drake stayed behind to be with Amber.

Jill had been in to visit her daughter briefly, but couldn't manage to see her that way for very long. She said a small prayer over her child, and placed a bible beside the bed. She was supported by a nurse, who escorted her back to the waiting area with Drake and the kids.

"I want to be with my children, but I can't leave Amber alone. I have to be here if ..." Drake caught himself. ... "When she wakes up."

"I understand. The kids will be fine. Just take care of my baby girl."

Drake kissed both of his children, and hugged them tightly, then watched them fade out of sight through the double doors. He had asked his mother-in-law to call him as soon as they made it home.

Chapter Fifteen

An Unexpected Guest

Paul hit I-70 the minute he heard about Amber's accident. Janie had called to cancel the two gym memberships, and Paul had answered.

"What hospital is she in?"

"St. Mary's, but you can't—"

Paul didn't let her finish the sentence. He thanked her and got off the phone. Until that moment, it hadn't registered with him just how strong his feelings for Amber were.

***

The double doors opened, and the same elderly lady who had greeted Drake stopped Paul in his tracks at the front desk.

"Sir, can I help you?"

"I'm here to see Amber Woods." He was careful not to reveal who he was, just in case.

"Are you family?"

"Um, yes, I'm her brother." Paul knew that in severe cases like Amber's, hospitals usually only allowed family members to visit.

He had a trusting face and was easy on the eyes, so the nurse let him through.

Once he reached the ICU, the other nurses outside Amber's room were smitten by his charm as well, and let him in to see her.

Paul entered the room quietly and with cautious steps. He took her by the hand, ever so gently, as he sat by her bed. It was hard to believe that the woman he saw before him was the same girl he had looked forward to seeing at 10am every day for the past eight months. The bruises on her face and arms were still prominent, along with the swelling.

He lingered for a few moments then turned to walk out.

***

In the hallway, Drake bumped into him. After almost a week of sleep deprivation, paired with the stress of the situation, Drake blew up at the unknown man who had just exited his wife's room.

"Excuse me, but who the hell are you?"

"Uh, I'm Paul. I'm Amber's yoga instructor." The intruder held out his hand.

"Yoga, huh?" Drake paused for a moment, then swung his fist and made contact with Paul's cheek. The blow sent him to the floor.

"Have you been sleeping with my wife, pretty boy?" Drake wrapped his hands tightly around Paul's shirt collar.

"Oh, you must be the self-absorbed, cheating-bastard husband I've heard so much about." Paul's comment was infused with condescension. A fight ensued, and the two men rolled around on the hospital floor. Each threw punches, as if their fists were playing a game of ping pong.

Hospital security came and broke the two men apart.

Paul wiped blood from the corner of his mouth. "I never slept with your wife, man."

"She wouldn't have me 'cause she's too hung up on you, not that you deserve it. Amber's a great girl, and if it weren't for you, she wouldn't even be lying in that hospital bed. Man, I'd give my left nut to have a woman like her, and don't think I'm the only guy who would feel that way."

Drake thought of going after Paul again for talking about his wife like that. But coupled with the fact that he was held back by two officers, and he knew what Paul had said was true, he shrugged away from the cops, and demonstrated that they had nothing more to supervise. The fight was over. The cops escorted Paul from the premises, and warned Drake to settle down if he didn't want to be next.

Drake assured the officers that he would behave. He walked down the hallway to clean up his face in the bathroom, and checked with the nurse to see if he needed stitches for his eye.

Chapter Sixteen

Waiting for a Miracle

For the next several weeks, Drake never left Amber's side. He had been in the hospital so long, that he was on a first name basis with all the nurses, but not in the way he would have been in the past. Now, they were relationships based on respect and gratitude for the care being given to his wife.

Each day, Drake would sit beside Amber's hospital bed and read the Bible his mother-in-law had left behind. Sometimes he'd read aloud to Amber, at other times, silently to himself. His favorite verse read:

'Therefore if any man be in Christ, he is a new creature; old things are passed away; behold, all things are become new.'

The passage gave him hope that things would be different, and it even made him believe that he really did deserve a second chance. When Drake wasn't at Amber's bedside, he could be found most often in the chapel, deep in prayer. He was definitely a changed man.

One of his daily rituals had become hand-washing and brushing Amber's hair smooth. She hated dirty hair, and although she wasn't aware of it at that time, he wanted her to be as close to her normal self as possible. There were times he'd even thought about putting makeup on her face, but always came back to realizing how beautiful she was, even without it.

Drake often imagined Amber's fingers moving or a toe wiggling, but the doctors always assured him "those were only reflexes."

He missed the children terribly and knew that they were feeling the same without either of their parents being around, so he called every single day to check in on them, and then again at night to listen to them say their prayers. When the phone conversations weren't enough, they chatted over video. He and Max even had simulated arm wrestles over the airwaves. He found it ironic that when he finally had time to devote to his kids, he couldn't actually be with them. As awful as it felt, he knew the kids realized that they were his top priority.

Every day he was faced with the same question from the kids, "How is Mommy today?" and each day his reply was the same, "Mommy is getting lots of rest so that she will have plenty of energy to tickle you both when she wakes up."

He hoped that fate wouldn't prove him a liar.

***

It had been six weeks to the day since Amber was admitted. Drake had used up all of his vacation time at work. Mr. Shelton tried to convince him to come back part-time to at least keep his insurance, but Drake insisted on staying with his wife. Thankfully, he had made some lucrative investments years ago, which he used to cover his living costs and pay the medical bills that resulted from the hospital stay. He had always taken care of his wife and kids, well … *financially*.

Drake actually felt relieved when he discovered that Mr. Shelton had replaced him.

Janie had been to visit Amber a few times, when Brad was home to take care of the kids. Drake put the house up for sale and hired a moving company to pack everything up, and transfer it to storage for a while. Janie was kind enough to supervise everything for him. She wanted to help her friend, and Drake's newfound commitment to Amber had made quite an impression on her.

He rented a hotel right next to the hospital, which allowed him to remain close in case any changes developed. And those makeshift beds had worked knots into his back. Occasionally, he tired of hospital food and went out for a burger or steak. But every day, without fail, he sat beside his wife's bed, stroking her hand, and praying over her.

***

Being a retired school teacher, Jill decided to home-school the kids. It provided a great distraction from the situation at hand. They did science projects and baked cookies together. Drake's children were in good hands, and he regretted not allowing them more time with their grandmother over the years. It was obvious that she adored them. He also thought about all the missed moments he and Amber could have shared, if only he'd had a better relationship with his mother-in-law.

One thing was certain, Drake was quickly realizing how much he had alienated Amber from other people in her life, and that he definitely had not offered a competent replacement.

Chapter Seventeen

Answered Prayers

Drake was asleep in the chair next to Amber's bed, holding her hand, when he felt something. At first he thought it was 'just another reflex' but he slowly raised his head to the most spectacular view he had seen in a while, Amber's green eyes. She was awake.

Still groggy and a little disoriented, Amber scanned the room. Not really focused on Drake yet, frantic, she asked about her children to the room around her.

"Where are they? Where are my babies? Annie? Max?" When she tried to sit up in the bed, Drake summoned the nurse, who administered an intravenous sedative to calm her down.

After using that momentary burst of energy, along with the morphine that quickly navigated its way through her veins, Amber became limp. Drake offered comforting words as he lowered her head back onto the pillow. "The kids are fine. They're with Jill."

He took a breath in, then said, "It's okay. I understand why you left."

When he saw she was drifting off again, he whispered, "Let's not talk about this right now. You need your rest, angel."

Drake watched his wife's eyes close as she succumbed to the sweet poison that was surging through her veins. He ran his finger over the top of her head and down her face, and then stepped outside to call Jill and Janie to deliver the great news.

***

When Amber awoke again, Dr. Davis entered the room to check on her. She still had a severe headache, so he ordered more morphine for her drip. Then he asked Drake to step into the hallway for a moment.

"Mr. Woods, your wife has been through a traumatic event, and we are very thankful she is awake, but she has a long road ahead of her. She's not paralyzed, but after being in a hospital bed for several weeks, she may have difficulty learning how to use her limbs again."

"I understand, Dr. Davis, and I'm here for whatever she needs."

"We'd like to keep her for a few more days for observation and run more tests, but if everything comes back clear, she will be able to go home soon. But before that, she has a lot of rehabilitation ahead of her."

Drake shook the doctor's hand and lingered in the hallway. *Home? Where is home now?* So much of his time and energy had been spent living moment to moment the past few weeks. His main focus was getting the kids away from that hospital to preserve some normalcy for them. Not much thought had been put into where they would all go when Amber was released. But, now that she was awake, there were decisions to be made.

He had already sold the house in New York, and they wouldn't have gone back anyway. Though he did regret how much Amber was going to miss her best friend. Drake didn't want to take another pleasure out of her life, but New York was no longer an option.

Before any major decisions were made, he had to ensure that Amber even wanted him back.

***

"I heard everything you said when I was in the coma." Amber spoke softly to her husband when he walked back into the room.

"You did?"

"I wanted to open my eyes, but I just didn't have the strength yet." She paused for a moment, and studied the bed sheet. "And I never cheated on you, Drake—though I had every reason to."

"I know, baby. Everything is going to be okay. I'm here, and I'm never leaving you again."

"You were here. I can't believe you stayed by my side every day."

He took her by the hand and traced the pale white circle where her wedding ring once rested. The staff had removed it before the operation.

"You're my girl and I love you … I promised you I'd always take care of you."

For the first time in weeks, Drake leaned over and kissed his wife on the lips. For a moment, Amber couldn't tell if what she was feeling was the morphine, or the fire in his touch. Deep in her heart, she knew it was the latter.

***

Amber rested off and on for the remainder of the day, which gave her the energy to greet her children when they arrived later that evening.

"Mommy!" The children squealed in delight as soon as they saw her face, despite the fact that their father had asked them to keep the noise level down in the hospital. They were so excited to see their mom awake.

He was able to prevent them from jumping on the bed, as he guided each one gently to their mother's side, and showed them how to touch her hand softly. Amber smiled up at him as she kissed the tops of her children's heads.

The nurses outside the room beamed as they watched the family reunite.

"Another miracle," one commented. "I wasn't sure if she was going to make it."

Then they returned to their duties.

Chapter Eighteen

The Road to Recovery

Amber spent the next six weeks in physical therapy learning how to use her muscles again. Drake was there every step of the way. He let her vent when she needed to, cry when she felt the pain, and celebrated every small victory with her.

Meanwhile, he had been on a recovery path of his own. He had not touched a single drop of alcohol since the night before Amber's accident.

The doctors ran a multitude of tests each day to check her reflexes, mental comprehension, and strength. She had finally gotten strong enough to leave the hospital, though she would still have to continue home therapy for the next four weeks. Things were slowly returning to normal—a new normal anyway.

Drake had Janie stay with Amber while he made a couple of trips out of town to handle some business. He had a job lined up and a few more surprises in store for her, once she was released.

***

On the last day, Janie greeted Amber at her hospital room door. She held a white gown, and it was definitely not the hospital type. The satin mermaid-gown had capped-sleeves, and a sweetheart neckline.

"What's this for?" Amber asked her friend.

Janie smiled. "Let me help you put it on. He's waiting."

Amber agreed and slipped into the gown with Janie's help. Her muscles were still a little sore, but she found a new burst of energy, due to the anticipation of what was transpiring. Janie brushed her friend's hair, added a little loose powder and lip gloss, and then escorted her out the door.

Drake waited in the hallway, and looked impossibly dapper, dressed in a gray pin-striped suit with a purple rose pinned to the lapel.

The children wore formal clothes, and stood either side of Jill. When Amber took a closer look, she noticed Janie was dressed formally too. What was going on?

Drake took her by the hand and placed a ring on her finger.

"Amber, I've spent a lot of years blind to the vision of perfection that you are. Not only are you the mother of my children and keeper of my soul, you are my best friend. I will spend the rest of my life making sure I am nothing short of your knight in shining armor. You are a princess and deserve the very best. You make me want to be a better man. I know I alienated you for a long time, for my own selfish reasons, but I've learned to live every moment of the day as if it were my last. I will use my last breath of life to let you know how much you mean to me, if you'll have me."

Amber cried when she looked down at the ring, and then around the room at all of her loved ones. It wasn't exactly as she had pictured her dream wedding, but in that moment, it was exactly what she wanted.

"But I already have a ring." Confusion masked her tears for a moment.

"I tainted that ring with my selfishness. This one signifies a new me, a new us. It's my promise to you that I will never be that man again."

Tears painted her cheeks. Amber accepted the ring and kissed Drake with every ounce of energy she had. It was even better than she remembered, and much hotter than the one she had pictured with Paul. Her husband could still make her melt inside. Oh how she had missed that feeling.

Then Drake gathered her things and helped her to the car. The surprises had just begun. A smile had plastered itself to his face.

***

Once on the road, Amber came back from her fairytale to the real moment. "By the way, where are we going?" She hoped he wouldn't say New York.

Before he could answer, she looked out the window and noticed they were heading west on I-70. She smiled and closed her eyes for what felt like only a few minutes. But when she awoke, they were passing a sign that said, "Welcome to Wichita."

About a half hour later, they pulled down a long driveway covered in gravel. Drake parked their vehicle outside a two-story brick house, with burgundy shutters, and bay windows in front. It was pleasantly familiar to Amber.

She looked over at Drake, flabbergasted. "What … how did you … I thought we sold the house?"

Drake smiled.

"We did. But I know how much you love it, so I contacted the owners, told them our story, and turns out, they were getting ready to sell it anyway. So it's ours again."

With a sudden, newfound energy, Amber got out of the car and walked to the front door. She stopped when she noticed her children's handprints embedded into the paver stones. Her fingers traced the tiny outlines.

As she stepped into the doorway, her eyes lit up. She contemplated all of the possibilities for redecorating. Her house was a clean slate, which mirrored her life at that moment. It was a rejuvenating feeling.

Drake unloaded the kids from the car, and carried the stuff from the hospital inside. He laid the items on the table then made his way over to Amber. She returned his embrace when he wrapped his arms around her waist from behind.

"What about the job in New York?" She turned to face her husband.

"Mr. Shelton found someone else to run the team. That job wasn't right for me anyway."

"But, how will we live? I can't go back to work, and I really enjoy being home with the children."

"I got my old job back, and I will be working from home making the same salary as before, but with the potential to be promoted within six months. Regardless, I'm not worried about it. We have plenty saved to back us up if we need it."

His words were reassuring. Amber was right about one thing, her husband was always good with money, and they never suffered financially.

As she wandered from room to room taking in the memories, Amber noticed that Drake had assembled the couple's bed in the master. *How does he do it?*

***

Later, Jill dropped by to take the kids to her house for the night to allow the couple some much needed rest. Amber was saddened by the thought of being away from her children, but she finally agreed. Soon after the kids were gone, Drake told his wife to go lie down and rest while he ran some errands. Again, although reluctant, Amber agreed.

***

Before Drake stopped by the restaurant, there was one place he had to visit, the florist. He grabbed a dozen purple roses, and one mixed bouquet then continued on his way.

***

His truck moved slowly and hesitantly, as he rolled by the sign that read, *Ever After Gardens*, until it finally came to a stop. It was his first visit to the site since the accident. He thought his presence would have caused the Smith family more pain, had he shown up at the funeral all those years ago.

Drake turned the ignition off and released a heavy sigh. Then he scooped up the bouquet of mixed flowers, and set a slow pace as he walked over to the headstone.

The boy's parents had done a great job on the design. It read: *Deacon Tanner Smith 1991 – 2003*, and had an image of a young boy holding a baseball glove and bat. Drake found out after the accident that Deacon enjoyed playing baseball. He knelt down by the stone, and placed the flowers on top. Then he pulled a small bible from his pocket and read these words:

"But Jesus said, 'Let the little children come unto me and do not hinder them, for to such belongs the kingdom of heaven.'

Matthew 19:14"

He closed the bible, and the words that followed came straight from his heart.

"Deacon, I am so sorry that I took you from your parents. I'm sure they miss you a great deal, but I realize you are now in a better place. No harm can come to you, no sadness, and no pain. I truly hope you are enjoying your new home in heaven … and having a blast playing baseball with the angels. They are a lucky bunch to have you."

A tear betrayed him as he continued.

"For a long time, I felt that I didn't deserve to be a father, because I took your parent's child away from them. But now I realize that not being there for my kids is only punishing them. The best way I can honor your memory is to be the best father I can be to my children, in the little time we have left together. I intend to make every moment count. Rest in peace, son, I'm sorry we met the way we did."

Drake sat for a few more moments and finally let go of all the sorrow and pain he'd been holding in all of those years. Soon he felt cleansed, forgiven, and for the first time in a while, at peace.

He stopped only once more on the way home to pick up dinner.

***

Drake was surprised to find all of the lights off when he arrived home. As he turned the key in the front door, he heard an old familiar song playing. The ultra-talented Percy Sledge belted out 'When a Man Loves a Woman.' He followed the sound to the master bedroom and found Amber waiting, and wearing nothing but a smile.

"I took a shower and couldn't find a thing to put on." Her smile was teasing and dirty.

Drake mirrored her gesture. "I think you made an excellent choice."

Then he took her in his arms and kissed her lips, passionately and with force. For a moment, he forgot that she might still be in pain. He paused, only to be met with Amber's arms, as she pulled him closer and tighter to her body.

"Don't stop." Her voice sounded ragged and needy.

She ripped open his button-up shirt and kissed a path from his neck down to his belly button. She paused only to unbutton his pants and lower them to the floor. Her eyes hungry, her skin on fire.

She looked up at Drake as he helped her stand. He picked up his lady and carried her to the bed.

Drake gently covered her body with his, atop the down comforter that felt like clouds against their skin. Amber's pulse raced and it matched their broken breaths. Kisses were delivered hard and fast, with an aching need. He ran his fingers through her soft auburn hair, then downward on her neck, and lingered for a moment on her voluptuous breasts. They felt amazing. It was as if he was touching his wife for the first time. His hand continued down the outer edge of her waist and hips, and then moved inward. All the while, Amber rediscovered every inch of his body with her lips, tongue, fingers, and any other body part she could use to make contact with him.

Not wanting to misunderstand her pain level, Drake asked, "May I?"

Desperation laced Amber's reply, "I want you so badly."

The passion continued, as they mirrored each other's movements—kiss for kiss, touch for touch, and breath for breath, until the moment finally came and they *fell* together.

They stayed tangled in each other's arms for the duration of the night, and enjoyed the most peaceful sleep they had both experienced in years. Neither of them turned away from the other even once during the night.

***

Amber awoke before her husband the next morning. She tiptoed out of the room and closed the door behind her. As she sauntered through the house enveloped by her robe, her mind contemplated all the past events that had taken place there. A smile invaded her face when she envisioned all of the new memories to come.

Last night had been the most passionate encounter she had ever experienced with her husband. Even an interlude with Paul wouldn't have been likely to hold a candle to her satisfaction.

She made her way to the back patio, sat on the steps, and watched the sky perform. A dark cloud moved further away, and the sun once again showed its face. She thought about her children, her husband, and all she had been through since the first tragedy struck, and then again during the recent accident.

Her life had come full circle, and she was finally right where she was meant to be all along. She had learned that when darkness breaks the soul, it can feel as if there are no options; that no one could understand or fix the pain, and life will always be a series of shadows. But, when the time is right, the sun will reappear to guide the way.

She had survived the darkest moments of existence and made it through to the other side, no longer broken, no longer afraid, and stronger than ever before.

QUESTIONS OR COMMENTS?

This was my first published adult fiction writing. Typically, I write children's books and parenting books. If you have any questions or concerns about this book or any of my titles, feel free to email me at tsanderspublishing@yahoo.com.

One Last Thing ... If you enjoyed reading this book and feel others would enjoy it too, please consider going to Amazon, search for my book title or my name, and leave a review. BE SURE TO CLICK ON THE BOX THAT SAYS, "Would you like the viewers to see that this was a verified Amazon purchase?" I would greatly appreciate your feedback.

Thanks for your support!

Acknowledgements

I would like to take this opportunity to thank a few key people who helped make this book possible. Without these awesome supporters, this novel would be nothing less than a saved Word document on my computer.

Alicia McDaniel: Thank you for your tireless efforts as my primary beta reader. You stuck with me from beginning to end and helped me ensure that the story flowed, that the characters were relatable and engaging, and that I even chose the right names for some of them. Thank you for helping me choose the title. I can't imagine this book being called 'Losing Jake' now, LOL. It's just wrong!

Most of all, thank you for being brave enough to be honest with me to help make my writing better. You are an awesome sister and I love you!

Rebecca Krawcewicz: Thank you for choosing to read my book over anything else in your life at times ☺ You know what I mean. You helped my scenes come alive with your word suggestions and descriptions. This was my first adult fiction piece and it was even more special than I imagined it would be, because I was able to share it with you, as a sister and a fellow avid reader. I love you so much and appreciate you taking the time out of your busy life to help me make this book a reality!

Harmony Kent: Thank you for giving me a 3-star rating on this book when you first read it. Your review was not just a run-of-the-mill 3-star rating. The words you used to describe my story built up my confidence and made me want to make it better. You didn't tear it down; you helped me see how much potential it really had.

Thank you also for agreeing to be my editor and making my story shine. You didn't turn my efforts into your own; you simply showed me how to enhance my words. I am extremely proud of this story now and have learned so much about writing and editing from you. I'm forever in your debt!

Thank you to my readers for giving my ideas a voice and my characters a chance to come alive. I hope you enjoyed Amber and Drake's journey as much as I enjoyed creating it.

As a special thank you, I am including the first three chapters of my next novel, 'Unsevered'. I hope you enjoy Harley and Jewel's story as much as Amber and Drake's. It definitely took **me** a while to be able to move on. ☺

Dedicated to all military spouses ... especially those whose loved ones made the ultimate sacrifice.

Unsevered

Traci Sanders

CHAPTER ONE

One.

One more brush of his skin on mine.

One more taste of his kiss.

One more wisp of his breath in my hair.

People say they would give anything to have 'just one more' moment with a loved one lost. That's not good enough for me. I want it all back. How could I be satisfied with *just one more* fleeting moment with the only man I've ever loved – the one who owns my soul … and will forever?

I can't let go.

* * *   * * *   * * *

The silence in my room is broken by the rattle of capsules in a little green bottle I hold in my trembling hand. I blink and hot tears stream down my face.

Two of these magic pellets can give me the sleep my body is craving, but a handful can bring me eternal relief from the agonizing pain ripping my heart to shreds. They may even take me to meet Harley.

Dad is busy with his new wife and daughters. My best friends, Chelsea and Gretchen, are workaholics. Mom is the only one I worry about. She and I grew quite close during my teenage years when Dad was busy with work. Most mother-daughter duos fight during that stage of life, but we clung to one another, keeping each other safe. I begged her to buy a house close by when I moved away to college. She didn't want to give up her home. I understood that. It was the only house we'd ever lived in as a family.

Mom stayed with me for a few days after I got the news about Harley, but being the ever-stubborn, fiercely-independent person I am, I convinced her I was fine so she would go back home. I knew she couldn't afford to miss much work.

Settling into married life, I was happy to spend all my time with Harley. Now he's gone. There's a void in me that no one can fill, not even my mom.

I stare into the bathroom mirror, but I don't like what I see. My puffy eyes are heavy with bags. No amount of concealer can hide the frown lines I've earned the past few days.

I shuffle to my bed and place the bottle on my night stand. I grab Harley's pillow and press it to my face; the faint traces of his cologne still remain. His watch rests where he left it. He said he didn't need it because, "It will be as if no time has passed when we see each other again. We'll pick up right where we left off."

Liar.

Chelsea and Gretchen – my best friends from college – live less than thirty miles from me, and they use that phrase too. We make plans to get together often, but it rarely happens. We maintain our feigned satisfaction with the situation by saying, "I haven't seen you in forever, but it's like no time has passed." We're going in different directions. No matter how good the intentions, life changes things.

I sniff a time or two and wipe my cheeks again. My hands shake as I grab the little green bottle one last time. I dump a few pills into my hand, and then add several more for good measure. I reach for my water bottle and prepare to toss back several of them. One for each memory I can't erase. I close my eyes and pray it won't take long for me to get to him. *I'm so sorry, Mom.*

Just as the first pill is about to meet with my tongue, the radio comes on by itself and plays a soft version of *"I Got You Babe."* My nose is invaded with the scent of Eternity cologne and a disembodied voice sends chills down my spine.

"Don't do it, Jules."

* * *　　* * *　　* * *

I would know his voice anywhere. "Harley? Oh, Harley."

"Yeah, baby. It's me. I'm here," he says, his words calm and soothing.

A tremble reverberates throughout my body. The tears seem to pause midstream on my face. My voice is barely audible.

"Where? I can't see you. I must be dreaming."

"No, you're not dreaming. You're grieving. And you're about to make the biggest mistake of your life."

If my hands were shaking before, they are almost convulsive now. Even my veins quiver at the sound of his voice. I wipe my eyes and run my fingers forcefully through my hair a few times. I slap my cheek to make sure I'm really awake. It hurts. *Yes, definitely awake.*

My inner thoughts escape through my mouth.

"This can't be happening. You're dead. I'm just hallucinating. It's the pills. Just the pills." I nod my head a few times with vigor to confirm it to myself. I look down at the bottle still in my hand; I haven't taken them yet. I put the capsules back in the bottle and close the lid.

"I've been watching you since the moment I died. I know what you were about to do."

My eyes shift toward the floor.

"But what's the use in living if I can't be with you? At least we could be together this way."

"It doesn't work like that, sweetheart. You can't kill yourself to be with me. We won't end up together."

Tears flood my eyes. "But I miss you, Harley. I want to be with you. There's nothing here for me anymore. I don't want to live without you."

The room is silent for a moment. I call out his name to ensure he's still there. Moments later, he speaks again.

"I know. I miss you too. But I lived out my destiny. I died doing what I was meant to do. I served my purpose in the world, and then I was called home."

"But your home is here with me. You belong here!" Anger and desperation seep through my words.

"The universe is done with me, but it isn't done with you yet, baby. You haven't fulfilled your destiny."

"And what is *my destiny*?" My tone is sarcastic. I walk around the room, grasping air, trying to touch the voice I'm hearing.

"I can't answer that for you; only you can discover it. But I know you're going to do great things in your world."

"I don't want to live out my destiny without you. We were supposed to be together forever, remember? We're, *unsevered.*"

My sobs return the minute that word escapes my lips. My mind slips into a memory of the day I first heard it. We'd just returned from our honeymoon and Harley said he wanted to go for a drive. He loved to surprise me, so I had no idea what awaited me.

* * * * * * * * *

Harley adjusted the blindfold he had placed over my eyes moments before. "Uh-uh, no peeking," he said. I smiled and pictured his dazzling blue eyes flickering with pure delight, the way they always do when he's happy or excited.

I threw my head back, lost in the moment, as a warm breeze danced across my face, offering the sensation of a dozen butterflies hovering in search of a soft place to land.

The 1965 Chevrolet Malibu eased down a bumpy, winding road, and finally stopped.

"Okay, we're here," he said.

Harley slid the blindfold off my eyes and a strong scent of salt air invaded my nose. The ocean!

I scrutinized the view and absorbed the magic. Endless sand was veiled by beautiful, white seagulls.

The waves performed a melodic tune as they covered the shore.

The beautiful Victorian beach house was more spectacular than anything I could have conjured in my imagination. It was a subtle taupe color, with windows that released outward at the bottom, allowing the ocean breeze to drift throughout the house.

My feet shuffled to the front porch and lingered on each pristine step before I reached the door. In a mesmerized state, I jumped when Harley's arms wrapped around my waist.

"Do you like it baby?"

"Like it? Harley, I love it!"

"Well, don't you want to see inside *our new home*?" His smile was wide, his eyes teasing. "Consider it a belated wedding present from my Uncle Walter."

"What?"

"Remember, I was his favorite nephew. He always told me it would be mine if…"

I didn't allow him to finish his sentence. "Oh no, he died! When?" I was frantic for a moment, worried about Harley losing his favorite relative and experiencing a pain from being lied to by my husband, by omission, anyway.

He laughed. "Calm down. He didn't die. He just decided to move into a smaller place to avoid the upkeep. He sold it to me for a very fair price."

I slapped his chest in a playful manner. "Don't scare me like that." I took another look around and said in a breathy voice, "Well, it's a heck of a wedding present. Remind me to send him an exceptional thank-you card. It's beautiful."

His gaze shifted toward the ground. "I hope it brings you some peace and comfort while I'm away."

His words were gentle but pierced tiny holes into my heart just the same. My lower lip quivered and I reminded myself to breathe; that we still had time. To my relief, Harley changed the mood with one of his typical 'glass-half-full' suggestions.

"Let's not talk about that. We're here together now, and I want to enjoy every minute with my wife." He pulled me close and covered my still-trembling lips with his.

I let out a squeal as he hoisted me into his arms and carried me over the threshold into our new home. I cupped my hand over my mouth and eased out of his arms to soak in the spectacular view.

The first space I entered was a massive living room, with immaculate, hardwood floors from wall to wall, and vaulted ceilings. An elegant, winding staircase to the left was covered in plush, beige carpet. The windows were veiled by sheer, white curtains, which allowed privacy without masking the view of the expansive ocean background. Not that it mattered much since, "There are no neighbors within a few miles of us," Harley informed me.

I sauntered to the kitchen on the right and slid my fingers across the marble island countertop that was lined by four swivel-backed bar stools. The appliances were custom-designed to match the chocolate-colored marble and a wine glass holder rested above the island. It was just like the one in a magazine I had shown him not long ago. He'd obviously paid attention.

I walked from room to room, upstairs and down, and discovered cleanly-designed spaces with no overpowering floral or striped patterns. It was exactly how I would have designed it myself, and I was impressed my husband already knew me so well.

I turn to Harley with narrowed eyes. "You did all of this?"

"Well, I had a little help. Our friends pitched in."

"How did you have time? These are all the things from our apartment?"

"It wasn't easy. I had to enlist some professional help to get our furniture moved out of our apartment while we were on our honeymoon. As far as the painting and decorating, you were pretty busy with planning the wedding so I was able to work on it in the evenings and some on the weekends. It really helped when you went on that spa retreat for a long weekend with your bridesmaids."

"And I was wondering what you were going to do to keep busy while I was away," I replied with a chuckle.

I continued to inspect the house and walked toward the glass doors situated off the living room. I stood on the back porch, facing the ocean. The warm mist from the sea sprinkled my skin. It became my favorite part of the whole house.

As I walked back inside, I saw a sign above the front entrance. It read, 'UNSEVERED'.

Harley noted the confusion etched across my face, placed my hands in his and said, "It means we will never be apart in spirit, even if we're somehow separated physically."

The room was silent. A tear threatened to escape my eye, but relented when a sense of desire washed over me. I looked deep into his eyes.

"Take me," I said. "Take me now."

Needing no further convincing, he placed both my cheeks in his palms and kissed me as we lowered our bodies to the stairs together.

Our eyes remained locked on each other and our tongues danced with strong intention. In between hard, fast kisses he said, "I love you so much, Jewel. I want to make love to you."

"I want ... your mouth ... all over me, Harley." My reply was breathy and needy.

He didn't even stop to take off my sundress, lifting it from the bottom instead. His strong hands traced a fierce path over the outer edges of my hips as his thumbs moved downward, squeezing and teasing my inner thighs.

"More. More." I didn't want him to stop.

A snapping sound startled me. I let out a high-pitched squeal as he tore the white lace of my thong underwear with just one hand, too impatient to pull it down. He'd never been this forceful, but I liked it. A lot.

He released one of my breasts from the top of my low-cut dress, and teased my hardened nipple with his tongue. I gasped, taking in the scent of pure virility ... mixed with a hint of Eternity cologne. The combination drove me crazy. I wanted him, all of him.

He moved upward for a moment to attack my neck, leaving teeth prints along the path. I gripped his hair with both hands and threw my head back in pleasure. His lips were velvet on my body, anywhere he chose to place them. My hands traveled downward in search of the button on his jeans, which held my prize. I released the gathering and pushed his pants and boxers to the floor, using only my foot.

My back found the stairs as he entered me, and I was more than ready. He pulled me close and I took him in and out again. One of his hands became tangled in my wavy, beige-blonde locks while the other gripped the banister rail in hopes of containing his early release. "Oh … Baby … you're … amazing!"

The passion was almost tangible – our breaths heavy, our skin on fire. A bead of sweat rolled off his forehead onto my breast. The ocean waves provided a blissful soundtrack to our ecstasy.

Almost too soon, the moment we were both waiting for came … but with great satisfaction on my part. Harley smiled and closed his eyelids as he produced short, weighty breaths. Exhausted, we both slid down the stairs at a careful pace, holding each other and basking in the afterglow.

Our short-lived encounter was more than made up for as we spent the remainder of the weekend christening every room in our new home.

* * *   * * *   * * *

My mind returns to the moment and I scold Harley's apparitional presence for lying to me. "You told me we'd be together forever. You told me that's what the sign meant."

"I did say that. But it didn't mean we'd be together forever in the physical sense; just that we'd always be in each other's hearts." His voice lowers and adopts a serious tone. "But there is one problem."

"What problem?"

"I am kind of stuck right now."

"What do you mean stuck?"

"Well, I was supposed to move on to my afterlife, but I can't do that until you let me go."

"But how do I do that?"

"I can't answer that for you. It's something you have to discover for yourself for me to be able to complete my journey. I'm sorry you feel like I let you down, but I did what I had to do."

A long pause cuts through the air for a moment. "I don't blame you, Harley. I know you didn't choose to leave me. I just miss you. Why can't I see you?" My voice keeps cracking as I wipe my tears for the umpteenth time.

"You'll see me when the time is right; when you are ready. And you won't be able to see the gift I left you until the time is right either." He was still surprising me, even in death.

"I'm ready! What is it? Please, I need something to hold on to."

"When you are ready to see it – and me – you will." He was beginning to sound like a broken record. "I have to go now, but I will be watching over you always. Please be kind to yourself and don't do anything else to endanger your life. Live. Be happy. Fulfill your destiny. And remember, I love you."

"I love you too, baby. Don't go." My voice is brittle, fading.

He doesn't respond.

"Harley?" I call out his name until my throat becomes scratchy and my voice is almost absent.

"Harley? Harley? Come back. Please don't leave me again."

There's no reply.

He's gone.

CHAPTER TWO

My body is locked in a sitting position on the bed for a few moments after I no longer heard Harley's voice.

My eyes scan the room until I spot a picture on the wall. I walk over and remove it from the hanger. It shows an image of Harley and I smiling, both red-faced from the alcohol we drank that night – and the fact that my friends had caught us making out when we'd just met. Damn smart phones are always handy.

I run my fingers over the picture and close my eyes as I recall the events of that night.

* * *　　* * *　　* * *

I was hanging out with Gretchen and Chelsea during karaoke night at a local bar. They dared me to find a male partner to accompany me on stage to sing *"I Got You Babe"* by Sonny and Cher.

"I'll do it with you," said a voice from behind me.

I turned and saw a striking, olive-skinned specimen of a man. He had chestnut-brown hair and piercing blue eyes. His no-doubt, chiseled abs begged to be sprung from his midnight blue U.S. Air Force uniform.

His face turned a crimson red as he stammered and backtracked. "I mean, I'll *sing* with you … if you want."

Heat rose to the surface of my face as he took my hand and escorted me toward the stage. Though I'm sure the tequila I'd enjoyed earlier played a part in my color-changed flesh, deep down I knew it was the electrical current that surged through every channel in my body at his touch.

My heart attempted to talk me out of it right away, reminding me I shouldn't go down that road again. I shouldn't allow myself to care about another man who might one day leave me.

I was pulled from those self-abusive thoughts when the man who was still holding my hand said, "I'm Harley, by the way. Don't worry. I don't bite … much." He winked at me and my body sizzled in places I didn't even know existed.

"Jewel. Nice to meet you, Harley," I replied, stumbling through every syllable. As we made our way to the stage, I turned and mouthed to my friends, "Oh my God." My heart was sending flares all over the place, but my flesh was drawn to that stranger by an inescapable force.

A few verses in, I discovered that he couldn't carry a tune in a bucket, but he sang his heart out as he devoured me with his eyes. I think the crowd may have sensed our undeniable chemistry as well, because they begged for a few more songs before we were allowed to escape the stage.

I wasn't ready for the night to end so we made our way to a table on the patio, away from the music and crowd. We sat and talked about everything under the sun. I first learned the basics. His favorite color? Blue. Favorite beer? Heineken. His favorite type of music was smooth jazz, but I would have guessed hard rock.

It could have been the beer talking, but deeper into the conversation he opened up, revealing darker things about his life. His mother died while giving birth to him and his father took his own life soon after, unable to deal with the pain of losing his one true love. Harley spoke of it in an almost scripted manner, as if he'd had to repeat it so many times before that he'd become numb to the emotional stigma.

"Oh, that's terrible. I'm so sorry," I replied. I had no clue how to respond to his words, so I started talking about myself to ease the tension.

"I've always had a pretty good relationship with my mom, but I can somewhat relate to not having a dad. Even when mine was there, he wasn't always present, if you know what I mean. He was covered up with work most of the time."

He offered a soft, empathetic smile and our conversation continued.

"So who took care of you when your parents died?" I asked as I scooped a mouthful of whipped cream off the top of my strawberry daiquiri. He smiled as he watched me lick it from the spoon.

"My mom's parents took me in. I was later told that my father's parents live on the west coast and aren't fond of kids, and that's why I didn't go live with them. They always sent me money on my birthday and Christmas, but I've never met them in person. How about you? What was your childhood like?"

"There's not much to tell. My life was normal, for the most part, until my parents told me they were getting divorced. On the night of my high school graduation, no less."

"Yikes, that must have been hard for you," he offered.

"Yeah, it was a huge shock, to say the least. They were good at playing their roles. I never saw it coming. They never fought, maybe because my dad wasn't around enough to fight."

I took a sip of my fruity concoction. I'd always felt a bit uncomfortable talking about myself, so I turned the questioning back on him again. "What was it like being raised by your grandparents?"

"Well, they always made sure I had what I needed, but I never felt comfortable there. I always considered it *their* home."

"So you felt like a stranger in your own home? That's so sad."

He cleared his throat and straightened his posture in an attempt to show his less emotional side, I suppose. He took a long chug of his beer as I awaited his response.

"Don't get me wrong. I wasn't deprived or anything. I appreciate everything they did for me. I mean, I had a roof over my head, my own room and went to a great school."

"But they didn't spend any time with you?"

He shifted a little in his chair. "They did, but only to teach me life lessons. My grandfather taught me things he thought would help me survive in life, like changing a tire, the proper way to hold a knife, how to use hand tools. My grandmother taught me how to do my own laundry and dishes, and attempted to answer any questions I had about women; not that I understand them any better, still to this day..." He threw an irresistible smile at me that warmed every vein in my body.

I returned the gesture and said, "Speaking of women, have you ever been married or come close to it? Any serious girlfriends?" The rum was making me braver by the minute. I was desperate to know everything about this man, and I especially wanted to know if I had any competition to contend with. Not that it would last long anyway. I'd been consistent on finding ways to screw these things up so far in my life.

"Not really."

It was a short answer but enough for me. I let out a small sigh of relief – hopefully not that he was aware of – and sipped my drink again to cool the fire that was igniting somewhere inside my body as I studied his chiseled face and burly physique. He caught me staring and I averted my eyes to the dance floor inside.

"I dated a few girls in high school but nothing serious. Never married. No kids. I enlisted in the Air Force right after graduating high school. I knew I wanted to be in the military all my life."

I admired the fact he wanted to follow his father's career path and make him proud, from *wherever* he was. When he mentioned the word 'kids', for some reason I found myself contemplating how much fun it would be to practice making babies with him. *God, we'd make pretty babies.* I reminded myself how to breathe as I attempted to tame the power that his azure eyes were gaining over my soul.

"But my grandparents mostly kept their distance unless I needed something. I think they may have blamed me for my mother's death." His eyes shifted downward immediately after those words escaped his lips. Embarrassment was written all over his face.

I placed my hand on his and felt that warm, electric tingle that I had come to relish already. I hadn't had much of a relationship with my grandmother, but I couldn't imagine a grandfather not doting on his grandchild.

"No, I'm sure that wasn't the case," I said, hoping to reassure him.

He offered a half-smile. "Well, the good thing was, since I stayed with them, I was able to spend a lot of time with my Uncle Walter, my mom's brother. He's the one who really took me under his wing. I learned a lot about life from him."

"Oh, like how to pick up women?" I teased. The warmth of his hand continued to mingle with mine.

"Not quite. I've never been 'good with the ladies,' so to speak," he said with finger-quotes in the air. But we had a lot of fun together. I used to stay at his beach house every summer. He taught me how to fish and catch shrimp. I love seafood. And he bought me my first *Playboy*."

I coughed, choking on my drink, and nearly spat it in his face. "Sounds like you two had a blast together." I laughed. "Your relationship with your uncle sounds a lot like the one I had with my grandpa – minus the magazines, of course. I spent summers with him as a kid. We did some of those same things. I was his only grandchild, so he kind of spoiled me."

"Ah, and did he teach you how to break all the little boys' hearts?" His eyes were wide and teasing, but I could tell he really wanted to know if he stood a chance with me.

"I haven't had much luck in the 'love' department either." I returned the finger-quote gesture to him. Then my eyes shifted downward as I continued, "Plus, when I started high school, I got busy with life and didn't visit him as often. I got word that he died during my freshman year of college." Harley's hand was tight upon mine now. I suspected he was taken back to the moment of losing his father. Perhaps our broken pieces would fit together enough to make at least one of us whole again.

"I'm so sorry. That must have been difficult for you. How did he die?" Harley asked.

"Throat cancer, which was ironic because the man never touched a cigarette in his life. Of course, he never let on to me that he was sick. I couldn't even attend the funeral. I blamed it on a major mid-term ... but in my own childish way, I guess I figured if I didn't say goodbye, he wouldn't really be gone."

"We all cope in our own ways. Joining the military was mine." A darkness lurked behind his eyes when he said that. He rubbed my hand and began to ask, "Jewel, would you..."

His words were cut short by the bartender shouting out for last call. I was already intoxicated – not by the alcohol, but by the beautiful stranger who had just penetrated my life with so little effort.

His eyes met mine again and he continued. "Can I call you sometime?"

I hesitated before answering, "Harley, I think you're great and I've had an incredible time with you tonight..."

"But…," he replied and cut me off.

"I'm not sure I'm right for you. Whether by choice or fate, all the men in my life abandon me." I paused for a moment and noticed him searching my eyes for more. I explained myself further. "So I start out every relationship just assuming it'll happen again. I leave before they do to avoid the inevitable."

He took both of my hands in his and our eyes performed an unspoken dance. "Jewel, I understand you being afraid of people you care about hurting you, but don't I at least deserve a chance to prove you wrong before you make up your mind about me?"

I stared into his crystal blue eyes and something inside told me I was safe with him.

He must have noticed I was wavering, because he asked, "Can I call you tomorrow and just go from there?"

After a couple more seconds, and the club owner's final threat to throw us out, I said, "Okay, I'll give it a shot, but don't say I didn't warn you." I wrote down my number on a napkin. What was I doing?

As my arm stretched out to hand him the paper, he pulled me in so close the pounding beneath the breast of his uniform turned my knees to mush. It matched the rhythm of mine. I tilted my head, leaned in to give him the green light and he placed his lips on mine. They were soft and full. His lower lip pulled my top one in with just the right amount of force—soft yet strong. Whether it was the level of alcohol still in my system or the intense fire that was burning in the lower part of my body, my inhibitions disappeared. I allowed him to explore my mouth deeper with his tongue. He was an amazing kisser.

My hands made a furious path through his brown locks as his became tangled in my tresses. No words were needed. Our bodies were so close that a dollar bill wouldn't have had room to slide in between. We finally pulled apart as the bartender kicked us out to close up for the night. That's when my friends yelled "hot stuff," and we turned around just in time to have our picture snapped.

My girlfriends grabbed me by the arm and pulled me toward the door.

"I'll call you!" he yelled across the bar.

Thank God Gretchen had stayed sober enough to drive. I was drunk … drunk in love.

* * *   * * *   * * *

My body shuddered when I saw his name come across my cell phone the next day. He had broken the mandatory three-day-wait guy rule, which was fine with me. It's a stupid rule anyway.

We began spending all of our days – and nights – together. I told him more about my parents, my grandpa, and how I went straight into college after graduation, where I majored in English and minored in journalism.

"How did you become an author?" he asked, as we sat in the *You'll Love it A-Latte* café one night.

I sipped my frothy drink then said, "When I graduated college, I got a job as a writer for a local newspaper. Later I started writing articles for an online magazine. It was mostly descriptions for fashion accessories, but it paid the bills and helped me strengthen my writing skills."

Now it was my turn to shift around in my seat, having divulged so much personal information about myself.

"So how long after that did it take you to get published?"

"I wrote my first novel when I'd been working for that company for about three years. I started looking around for an agent, but it was a grueling process. I must have gotten thirty rejections before I finally found one who took a chance on my work. It's true what they say about authors needing to develop a thick skin. Even after I secured an agent, it took about a year for it to be released. But it was worth it because in less than three months, my book reached the top ten on the New York Times bestseller's list," I replied as my cheeks burned with embarrassment. I'd never been comfortable talking about my success as an author. It felt a bit self-indulgent.

"Impressive. What was it about? Anything I would have read?" he asked with a teasing smile.

"Not likely," I said with a chuckle. It was a fantasy romance titled 'Beyond the Stars.' "

"Yeah, that doesn't sound like something I would have had laying around the barracks," he replied with a hearty laugh.

Our conversations got deeper over the next few months. I learned everything there was to know about him.

Even more, I told him everything there was to know about me. Something about him made me convince my heart that it was safe with Harley.

He would never abandon me.

He was different.

He was *the one*.

*** *** ***

I place the picture back on the wall and shuffle to the right to view the next one. It shows Harley and me standing on stage in a side embrace. I'm showing off my princess-cut diamond ring.

He'd just proposed, and to my own surprise, I said yes. That night unfolds in my head for a moment. I can almost hear the music playing in the background at the *Mango Tango* club where we first met.

*** *** ***

I cheered along with the crowd when he took the stage and belted out his rendition of *"Shameless"* by Garth Brooks. God help him, he loved to sing.

When the song ended, he dropped to one knee and informed the audience that he had a little announcement to make. His eyes met mine and it was as if there was no one but the two of us in that crowded room. My breath abandoned my body when I heard his words:

Jewel,

I've gone through my entire life not knowing the love of parents or siblings, and feeling as if I never really belonged anywhere. But that all changed when I met you. You have shown me more love than I could have ever imagined possible.

You've become my best friend, my lover, my safe haven. I would give my last breath of life to keep you safe and keep that light shining in your eyes that guides my heart. You bring out the best in me and make me want to be a better man. I finally know my place in this world—it's right here by your side. Please do me the honor of becoming my wife and allowing me the chance to show you every day for the rest of my life just how special you are to me. Will you marry me?

My hands shook and mascara-tinged tears soaked my face. I joined him on stage with a kiss and a resounding "Yes!" as his trembling hands slid the ring onto my finger. The whole building roared with applause and whistles. The club owner took our picture and even gave us a copy. We later found out that he hung it on the wall in the club. It was an unforgettable night.

*** *** ***

My tears flow without mercy now as I hug the picture for a moment then hang it back on the wall to take down another one—our wedding day. It was just as wonderful as I'd always imagined it as a little girl. That memory slides to the forefront of my mind for a moment.

*** *** ***

White chairs were lined in neat rows, covered with white linens and purple sashes tied to the backs. It was an elegant scene.

My mom waited with me in the bridal dressing room while Chelsea and Gretchen finished some last-minute decorating outside. I was pacing and biting my nails, almost ready to call the whole thing off.

"Honey, are you okay?" she asked as she offered some last-minute hair fluffing.

"I don't know, Mom. I've never been married before. What if it doesn't work out?"

She shooed away the remark with a wave of her hand. "Why would you say such a thing? Of course it's going to *work out*. It's normal to be nervous on your wedding day. But don't worry, you and Harley are meant for each other."

I turned and looked my mother in the eyes. "Yeah, I thought you and Dad were 'meant for each other' too, but look how that turned out."

"Jewel, that was different. You and Harley are not your father and I." She paused for a moment and swiped a tear that threatened to leave the corner of her eye, and then straitened her posture to reinforce the validity of her next statement. "We were young and right out of high school. Getting married just seemed like the next logical step. Your father and I never dated anyone else. You're thirty years old and you've dated *a lot* of men."

"I'm just saying, honey, you and Harley dated other people before you met. You took the time to get to know one another, and you both established your careers early in life. The timing is perfect for the two of you."

I sat and expelled a heavy breath. She took a place beside me, used a half-bent finger to turn my eyes toward hers and said "Honey, don't punish Harley because of your feelings toward your dad. He loves you."

"Thanks, Mom. I hope Dan makes you as happy as Harley makes me."

Mom had recently met Dan at a *Parents Without Partners* dance she'd been dragged to by one of her colleagues. I'd noticed a light in her eyes that I'd not seen before.

She hesitated before releasing her next words. They must have been held in her heart for a long time. "He looks at me with such desire and affection. Your father never looked at me that way."

My mouth was agape. "Mom!" Then I laughed and said, "Well, I know of at least *one* time that he must have looked at you that way, because I'm standing here."

We both laughed at that, and it released the butterflies I'd been holding captive in my stomach the entire day. I was ready to get married.

* * *   * * *   * * *

My father walked me down the aisle. It was the first time I could remember ever having his undivided attention. His new wife Susan sat in a chair toward the front. He was the first to remarry after the divorce and I kind of blamed Susan for 'stealing' my father in the beginning. Of course, I grew up and realized that things didn't exactly happen the way I'd conjured them up in my mind. My parents assured me their split was mutual.

Since Harley was a Second Lieutenant, the ceremony was true-to-form military style with all the elaborate traditions. It was held in an open field near the base. My dress was gorgeous, capped-sleeved, satin, with a sweetheart neckline and flowy bodice. I carried a bouquet of purple and white roses. My veil was a simple circular flower arrangement with traditional tulle that cascaded down my back.

I was enamored to learn that the passage through the 'arch of steel', presented by his fellow soldiers, was meant to ensure our safe transition into our new life together. The reception wasn't quite as elaborate, but was perfect for us. We serenaded our guests with our notorious rendition of *I Got You Babe* to commemorate the day.

At last the night ended and we said our "thank-yous" and "goodbyes" then made our escape to Port Canaveral to board the *Lady of the Seas* cruise ship, destined for the Bahamas for the next seven days.

* * *   * * *   * * *

I hang the picture back on the wall and continue to stand there looking at all the others in our collection. There's one of us on the cruise ship, another with us snorkeling in the crystal blue waters of the Bahamas.

The one thing I made sure to do when we moved in was create an 'Our Story' wall, an idea I'd seen on Pinterest. I knew I wanted to have one in my own home someday.

I just never imagined our story would have ended so soon.

CHAPTER THREE

It's amazing how much one can miss taking care of another person. There's no extra laundry to be done, no dirty dishes to wash.

His clothes hang in perfect rows in the closet, his toothbrush sits dry and unpasted in its holder. I asked him three times if he'd packed it. Not that he needs it now.

Cruel reminders are everywhere that he's never coming back for these things, that he's never going to need them again. The joy and laughter that once filled our room mocks me now. What's there to look forward to anymore?

I curl up in a ball under the covers and breathe in what little of him remains on his pillow. Behind my tear-soaked eyes lurks a memory of our last day together when he was alive. It had started out as the perfect day.

* * * * * * * * *

Harley slept in as I tiptoed downstairs to make breakfast. In moments, the house was infused with the scent of bacon, eggs, French toast, and coffee. I enjoyed my food out on the back porch watching the waves caress the shore. I finished my meal, placed some fresh fruit in a bowl on the side, and carried the tray upstairs. He blinked his sleepy eyes when he saw me. His smile was intoxicating.

"Mmm, looks delicious." He sat up in bed with arms folded behind his head.

"Well, after last night, I figured you could use a little refueling." I offered him a dirty smile.

"The food looks good too." He returned my gesture, took the tray from my hands and sat it on the dresser. Then he grabbed me by the waist, and threw me onto the bed.

I squealed and squirmed around in hopes of escaping his strong fingers that were torturing my ribs. "No, stop! I hate to be tickled!"

"Ooohhh, let's find out if I can make you pee your pants," he teased, and continued to find other *reactive* areas.

Finally, I made my counterattack and managed to grab the bulging stones between his legs. I squeezed until the power in his fingers diminished and he surrendered.

"Ha, looks like I'm not the only ticklish one." I threw him a victorious smile, released his genitals, and fell onto my back.

He gently rolled on top of me and stared into my blue eyes. His soft fingers brushed through strands of my hair. "I love you, Jewel. I can't believe I'm lucky enough to get to wake up to you every day for the rest of my life. Thank you for marrying me and making me the happiest man alive."

"I love you too, Harley. You are the best thing that's ever happened to me and I'm proud to be your wife."

We locked lips, barely allowing a breath to escape. His hands began to wander and just as they reached my belly button, the phone rang.

Our passionate moment was replaced by silence as he answered it.

"This is Harley." He shooed me away from him and whispered "go away" with a smile, then, "No, Sir. Not you, Sir."

My husband's eyes adopted a gloomy appearance and he turned away to finish the conversation. I heard the words, "Yes sir, I will be there." And then a click.

Knots formed in my stomach and my breakfast threatened to reappear. I closed my eyes hard and the only sound I heard was the echo of my pounding pulse. I knew this time would come eventually, but didn't expect it to happen so soon.

No, no, no. It wasn't fair. We'd just returned from our honeymoon, hadn't even had our first fight as a married couple.

He hung up the phone, almost in slow motion and sat on the bed without a word; his head hung low, his breath heavy. He turned to face me and took both of my shaking hands in his.

"That was my commander. He said we pull out at 0600."

Tears pooled in his eyes. I'd never actually seen him cry and I wasn't sure how I would react if I did. I was sure I wouldn't be able to contain my own emotions, so I forced myself to play my part the same way I did when my parents told me they were divorcing. I shut down. My arms pulled away from his and I began to pack his things as I rambled.

"So what all do you need to take? Will it be hot there?"

I grabbed a few t-shirts and pairs of boxers. "How many pairs of socks do you think you'll need?"

I wanted to die inside with each piece I placed inside his duffle bag. My stride was broken for a moment as I paused to inhale the scent of one of his t-shirts. My body shuddered and tears streamed down my face. I wasn't able to fake it as well with him.

Harley wrapped both of his arms around my waist and placed soft kisses on the back of my neck.

"Jewel, honey. Look at me."

I restored my brave face and turned toward him with my eyes trained on his—determined not to let him see my tears. His muscles bulged against my skin with tension and he embraced me as if he never wanted to let go.

"It's going to be okay. We can get through this."

"I know. I'll be fine," I said, lying so easily.

Knowing that it might be quite some time before we would have the chance again, we finally rediscovered the mood and made love one last time. It was soft and sweet, the perfect way to say goodbye. Our bodies stayed pressed tight together for the rest of the night. I finally found rest, listening to the beat of his broken heart, because mine was playing the same tune.

The break of dawn illuminated the path as I drove Harley to the base. His head leaned against the passenger window, his eyes fixed on nothing particular as signs and trees whizzed by. I could tell he was torn between staying with me and doing the right thing, even though there was no choice to be made.

Almost in slow motion, we unloaded his things from the car and embraced, surrounded by the other soldiers who bid their own farewells to their loved ones.

The pain in my chest was unbearable. I tried to swallow the lump that had formed at the back of my throat as the last few soldiers boarded.

Harley brushed a half-bent finger along my cheek. "Remember the sign, sweetheart. I'll always be with you."

His voice was soft and empathetic, as he placed tiny kisses upon my hand. The plane engine roared a signal that takeoff was imminent. He pulled me to him and covered my mouth with his, and time stood still. Our tongues entwined as our wet lips slid across one another at a fierce, desperate pace. I'm not sure if either of us even breathed for the duration of that kiss. We shared a long, final embrace and then he joined his comrades.

I waited until the plane was but a dot in the sky to release my pain. Hot, stinging tears drenched my cheeks and became waterfalls within seconds. The other military spouses around me inquired if I needed anything. When I declined, they offered a supportive hand on my shoulder and gathered their children to head back home to continue living life the only way they knew how. Alone.

It took a few minutes to compose myself. I sat in the car for a moment, unable to move, unsure of what to do next. All of my actions and decisions had been guided by the strong and loving presence of Harley for the past year. Not that he was controlling, I just preferred to be with him more than anyone. He was gone … and I was lost. The ache in my chest was so violent I thought my lungs were going to explode.

At last, I wiped my warm face with my hands and turned the key to drive home, the home I was supposed to share with my husband.

If only I had known that would be our last moment together. I would have kissed him longer. I would have never let him go.

I remember coming back to this house and not wanting to face my first night alone, so I invited Gretchen and Chelsea to sleep over that night. We hadn't spent any time together since I'd returned from my honeymoon, and I figured some girl time would be good for me.

Our evening began with me giving them the tour of the house.

* * *　　* * *　　* * *

"Wow, it turned out really nice, Jules! The colors he chose are gorgeous," Chelsea said.

"Right, like you two didn't have a huge hand in this." I squinted at both of them.

"Well, we did move in some of your stuff from your old apartment and set up while you two were on your honeymoon, but Harley was adamant about choosing the colors and décor for the house. He was quite involved in the whole process," Gretchen said.

"Yeah, you got a good one there, Jules." Chelsea added, with an envious smile.

I spun my engagement ring around to line up the diamonds with the wedding band. *Yes I do*, I thought to myself.

I hugged them both and said, "Thanks, girls. You two are the best. I appreciate everything you did at the wedding and helping make my new home so perfect, even if I never said it."

"We love you, Jules," Chelsea replied. She brushed a bleached blonde curl from her flawless, made-up face.

"Yeah, we're happy for you and Harley," Gretchen added.

"I'm starved. How about Chinese?" Chelsea offered.

"Sounds good. I'll put on a movie," I replied. I ordered *"The Fault in Our Stars"* on my DVR and we all made preparations to settle in for a few hours.

Chelsea removed her hot pink Dolce & Gabbana pumps and set them to the side of the couch. Then her five-foot-nine Barbie frame with flawless blonde locks disappeared into the downstairs guest room to change out of her business attire.

Gretchen released her reddish-brown bun and ran her fingers through her hair as her just-shy-of-five-foot frame carried her to the bathroom to change.

Once we were all in our PJs, we noshed on eggrolls and wine, and laughed and cried throughout the movie. It didn't take long for me to regret having chosen a sappy love story because I was missing Harley more than ever by that point.

Afterward, we stayed up a little longer and talked, mostly about our college days.

"Yeah, Jules, you've got a good man with that Harley." Her words were slurred due to the massive amounts of wine we'd consumed by then. "You haven't always been lucky in the man department."

"What's that supposed to mean?" I said, letting out a giggle. The alcohol had reached me, too.

"Do you remember that guy you dated our junior year?" Chelsea asked. "What was his name? Scott, Todd, something like that." She snapped her thumb and finger together, as if that would trigger the correct name.

"His name was Tadd, thank you very much," I replied. "Why, what was wrong with Tadd?"

Both girls burst into boisterous laughter.

"Remember he wrote you that love song and sang it to you outside our dorm window that night?"

"Yeah. What about it? I thought it was sweet," I replied.

"Disgustingly sweet. That's what drove you crazy about him, remember?" Gretchen said. "How did that song go again?"

I shared the song with my friends.

Jewel, my Jewel

I'd be such a fool

If I ever let you go

I'd die, I just know.

"Now that I've recited it out loud, I see what you mean. That was pretty bad." I joined them in laughter.

"I don't think I've ever dated a guy who could sing in key," I said. "Good thing they have other talents."

Laughter erupted in the room with when I said that. We were all pretty wasted by that point. Merlot bottles and empty margarita glasses lined the coffee table, anesthetic concoctions to numb the ache in my heart, even if only for a little while.

Our night ended with all three of us passed out on the floor. It was a perfect way to spend my first night without Harley, but deep down, I knew it was a temporary fix.

We all got up around noon and enjoyed a light lunch together at my favorite local restaurant, Bistro on the Bay. When it was over, we hugged, promised to get together soon, and parted ways.

Sooner than I'd hoped, I was back at home, alone once again. It was thoughtful of Harley to have all our stuff moved in and set up, but at that moment, I had nothing to do but sit and wait out the loneliness. At least if I had something to decorate, clean, or unpack, I would have been able to keep my *hands* busy. Instead, I opted to focus on occupying my mind with writing.

The waves mocked me rather than brought me peace in that moment. I sat and wrote the only words that came to my mind, a letter to my love.

Dearest Harley,

*It's been less than twenty-four hours since we left each other's arms, and yet it feels like an eternity. I thought I would be stronger than this, and be able to face being alone, but already the vast emptiness is consuming me. It's like I've forgotten how to breathe without you next to me. I invited the girls over to help me get through the night. Funny, I used to look forward to hanging out with them every spare moment I had, but this time wasn't the same. It was fun, but I found myself wishing you were here with me instead. I realized that **you** have become my new best friend. You are now a part of me that I can't live without, and don't want to live without. I will be counting every second until you come back to me, but I will try to stay strong for you. I love you, and we will always be unsevered.*

Your wife,

Jewel

I couldn't send it. First, I had no address to send it to. Second, I wanted to be strong for him. I didn't want to make him feel guilty for choosing an admirable profession like serving his country. I folded the paper and slid it into an envelope. Then I placed it in my underwear drawer and turned out the light to face my first night alone in our bed, which seemed to extend for miles since he was no longer there to fill the space beside me.

Each night was a repeat of the one before. I stayed up as late as possible writing or watching television. Now that my friends had returned to their own lives, my characters were the only ones I could talk to. Once I reached the point of exhaustion, my feet shuffled up the stairs in hopes of a good night's sleep; but my dreams had other plans. They were always the same:

Harley is walking up the front steps. He's home! I rush out to meet him and just before we touch, a bomb is dropped in between us and he is blown away.

I jolted awake after the explosion. My breath was rapid and heavy and my sheets were soaked in sweat. I pushed my hair back and wiped my face. I grabbed his picture from the bedside table and kissed it, offering a silent prayer once again. Then I placed it back in position and attempted to finish the night.

For the next few hours, the waves mirrored my movements as they tumbled with lack of direction in the sea. I bolted upright again and looked around, awakened by what sounded like a thump at the door. I grabbed my flashlight and Beretta from the night stand drawer, and then took a careful stroll around the house to ensure all was in place. (Thankfully, Harley took me shooting a few times before we married to make sure I knew how to protect myself while he was away.) My heart pounded at such a fierce volume that I worried it would be a dead giveaway, no pun intended. I tiptoed through the house, checking every corner and closet, my hand trigger-ready. Nothing seemed amiss.

I expelled a heavy sigh of relief and returned the gun to its safe place. Then I walked back downstairs and drank some warm milk. My eyes continued to survey the house with each step I took.

Confident my home had been disturbed by nothing more than my own imagination, I returned to bed. My slumber remained as restless as the sea night after night, until that dreadful day came and confirmed that my nightmares had become my reality.

*** *** ***

At first I didn't pay much attention to the black car parked behind the soldiers who stood before me. They were accompanied by a chaplain and what appeared to be a paramedic, though at first I wasn't exactly sure why either of those individuals was necessary. It didn't take long to find out.

"Hello, Mrs. Decker. We apologize for waking you, ma'am, but we need to speak with you for a moment. May we step inside?"

"Of course, but I'm fine here on the porch. We can talk here."

The melancholic tone in his voice declared that something was wrong right away. My legs disappeared from under me and the two soldiers lowered me to the rocking chair. The lead officer returned to an upright position, forced a stoic expression on his face, and continued with his military spiel.

"I have been asked to inform you that your husband, Second Lieutenant Harley Decker, was reported deceased in Kabul, Afghanistan at 1845 on May 22, 2014. A missile struck his plane during an ambush. Several soldiers were killed during this attack and regrettably his was on that list of names." His voice cracked a little and he paused to regain his composure to complete his speech. "On behalf of the Secretary of Defense, we extend to you and your family our deepest sympathies for your great loss."

His tone and posture softened as he added, "Ma'am, on a personal note, Harley was a good soldier and friend. He will be sorely missed."

I was numb, unable to speak. My ears rang. A thousand thoughts flashed through my mind like a 9mm reel. Images of our wedding day ... the beach in the Bahamas ... him carrying me over the threshold ... our last moments together, making love.

Then the images changed as I imagined what he must have gone through in his last moments, the ear-splitting sound of missiles and his yells for help because of the excruciating pain caused by the flames on his skin. It was too much for my brain to process. My breath came at a rapid pace, but I forced it to slow so I wouldn't hyperventilate. I just wanted those men to go away, so I somehow commanded my mind to move on. There would be plenty of time to fall apart once they left. All I could hope for was that his death was quick and without unbearable pain. My eyes remained dry. I was too shocked to respond to what I'd just heard.

I wasn't sure if I had even replied to the young man, but I suppose I did because at some point, he returned to his car and drove off at a careful pace. He had offered to have a neighbor or family member come stay with me, but I informed him that there was no one to call, and I was fine. Of course, I lied. He also left a card with a number to call for more information about the incident. I didn't want to know anything else; I couldn't bring myself to even think about the other details. How much more did he suffer? I couldn't bear to find out.

I did remember him saying that the military would be in touch to discuss the arrangements for Harley's service. I also vaguely recalled him stating that there would be a remembrance ceremony.

It was as if my soul abandoned my body as I closed the door behind me. I fell to my knees and buried my face in my hands. My body rocked back and forth, as if music was playing in the background, but my sobs were the only sound that echoed throughout our empty house.

Mom came to stay with me for a few days. She, along with Gretchen and Chelsea, attended the service and tried to convince me to, but just as I'd done with my grandpa, I didn't want to be a part of it. I couldn't do it. Couldn't listen to the trumpet blaring out *"Taps,"* couldn't take having an officer placing that flag on my lap. People would have repeatedly offered the 'we're so sorry for your loss' speeches throughout the entire event. I know folks mean well and feel helpless in times like that, so they feel obligated to say these things; but none of it helps.

No amount of sympathy or condolence would bring him back to me.

For the next few days, I played my denial role well, and even convinced Mom I was well enough for her to go back home. *So I could grieve in solitude the way I preferred.* Gretchen and Chelsea had to get back to their jobs, thankfully.

When she left, I went back to doing what I do best during tragic times. I shut the world out. I functioned on auto-pilot. I couldn't eat or sleep, and barely moved throughout the day. Showers were not a concern to me.

One day, two soldiers showed up on my front porch with a box in hand. I sat on the couch, hidden from view, until the knocking finally stopped and my feet carried my small frame over to peek out the front window. Once the driver was out of sight, I opened the door and found a small box on the porch, with the name Second Lieutenant Harvey Decker written on top. I concluded that it contained his personal belongings. There was that neatly folded American flag on top. I slid the box inside, and sat it in a corner to deal with later.

I wanted to kick it across the room, but decided that would be disrespectful. So many emotions were swirling around in my head, anger, sadness, betrayal. I knew he didn't really betray me, but I couldn't shake the feeling that I had been cheated out of the life I was promised.

* * *   * * *   * * *

I sigh as my mind returns to the present moment. I toss the pills in the trash, angry at the realization that I'm much too chicken to take them.

When I reach the bottom of the stairs, I see the sign above the door and vent my anger to the empty room.

"So you're really gone? This is it? This is all I get? You sweep me off my feet in a whirlwind, and then leave me to live in this huge house all alone?"

My voice gets louder. "I don't want this fairytale without you!" I walk over to the sign, tear it from the wall, and sling it toward the patio doors with as much strength as I can muster. It doesn't break. *Damn weatherproof glass.*

'Unsevered' .... coming soon!!!

Again ... If you enjoyed reading 'When Darkness Breaks' please consider visiting Amazon and leaving a review to tell others about it. BE SURE TO CLICK ON THE BOX THAT SAYS, "Would you like the viewers to see that this was a verified Amazon purchase?" I would greatly appreciate your feedback.

Thanks for your support!